SYNTH

AN ANTHOLOGY OF DARK SF | EDITED BY CM MULLER | ISSUE #1 | MARCH 2019

Copyright © 2019 by CM Muller and Individual Contributors. SYNTH is published quarterly in St. Paul, Minnesota. For more information, please visit: www.synthanthology.wordpress.com

Surrogate | Dan Stintzi 1

Flow to the Sea | Steve Toase 19

House of War | Virginie Sélavy 35

Music in the Age of Sheep | Charles Wilkinson 51

CONTENTS

Aenvalit | Farah Rose Smith 79

The Transported | Jeffrey Thomas 97

Empathy | Christopher K. Miller 125

The Object of Your Desire Comes Closer | Joanna Koch 141

SURROGATE
Dan Stintzi

DAN STINTZI received his MFA from Johns Hopkins University and currently lives in Wisconsin with his wife and dogs.

EMMONS FOUND THE BODY BY THE RIVERBANK. HE SPOTTED

it by the color of the coat, a dark green against the white and gray of the snow and ice. There was warmth buried somewhere deep below the skin. He lifted the body, untangled its foot from the barbs of a rusted fence, and carried it over his shoulder, trudging back through his old bootprints. Inside, he set the body upright against the tree that had grown inside his home. The tree was dead now. Emmons tried to make the body speak again but it would not.

From his bedroom, he took the spare coats he had collected during the raids and piled them across the body until only the face was visible. He had seen the face move days before; he had seen it chew and breathe. But the cold had changed the body's appearance. Now the eyes were bruises, the mouth an open sore. The heat he had felt was gone. The boy was dead. He went out to find the mother.

The mother's name was Stena. She lived on the city's edge in a ruined schoolhouse. She hid knives in the old desks. She cracked stones and made chalk, wrote words and numbers on the blackboard. In this way, she had taught the boy to read. She had lived with Emmons some time ago but then the boy arrived and everything changed.

In the schoolhouse, Stena sat beside a fire pulling the skin off a rabbit. The tiny fibers that held the skin to the muscle would not separate so she weaved a knife sideways along the meat.

"I have something I need to show you," he said.

"I thought you weren't talking to me," she said.

"It's important."

"I'm in the middle of something here." The knife tore through the last thread and the skin came loose.

He was momentarily sidetracked by the scene, thinking of himself as the rabbit, wondering if his skin could be removed in the same way, all at once with a single strong tug. She drove a pointed stick through the meat and held it over the fire.

"I have bad news," he said. "I'm sorry."

"Spit it out," she said.

He told her. The fire cast new shapes on her face. Her eyes were black, orange, then black again. He went to comfort her with his hands but the place where she had been was empty. She was three buttons up on her parka, the hood over her head. Her face was gone. He followed her out the door and into the cold.

She did not take steps; she kicked through the snow with Emmons just behind her. His breath came in shallow waves. His heart felt too big inside his chest.

From the outside, Emmons's house looked as abandoned as the buildings that surrounded it. The windows had melted; the gutters were filled with ash. Stena knew how to access the crawl space hidden on the back side of the house, through the body of a hollowed-out minivan, past a washing machine on rollers, under the porch, into a tunnel of chiseled out foundation ending in a foot of half-frozen water slicked across the basement floor.

Up the stairs, in the room with the dead tree, Stena saw the body, which had somehow slumped over in Emmons's absence. She fell to the floor and cried into the moldy rug. The noise she made reminded him of a pheasant he had seen shot out of the air . . . not dead, screaming a bird scream, doing one-winged loop-de-loops—earthbound spirals—until it pranged headfirst into the trunk of a tree and fell silent.

During the time when they had shared this home, he had, as a kind of protest, made a point of ignoring the boy. It was Stena who decided they would offer him shelter. Now he straightened the child upright against the tree and used his thumb to close his dead eyes. The body had thawed while he was gone. The skin was a fish's skin. The color of it was gray and blue.

Stena had rolled over. She was staring up at the ceiling. The hood of her parka made her head seem engorged, grotesque.

"Where did you find him?"

He told her. She started making the shot pheasant sound again. He said: "What business did he have being down there?"

"I believed in him having freedom. I wish that he didn't go to the river but that was his choice and he made it."

The kid was dead and his eyes were closed, but Emmons still had the sensation of being watched. Stena stayed on her back. He followed her eyes and saw the snowy light through the holes in the ceiling. The light made him blink repeatedly.

"I need you to do me a favor," Stena said.

"No."

"You have to at least listen."

"I sure as hell do not. You lost the opportunity to ask me for favors when you left for that schoolhouse."

"My moving is irrelevant to the favor. My son is dead for Christ's sake."

"That is not your son."

"Oh, fuck you." She rolled back over and screamed at the floor.

"You keep that up and they'll find us."

The rug muffled her voice. "Those freaks gave up on me and you a long time ago."

The boy's body slumped sideways again. Snow began to fall through the holes in the ceiling. The light coming through the holes illuminated the sideways body like something in a painting.

Painting was a word that struck Emmons as strange sounding. He had forgotten what it meant, but the light, the body, the colorful coats all piled together, they moved his mind back in time and the meaning returned. Things fell out of use and were forgotten. He could not remember all the things that had gone away.

"If I come back will you do this for me?" she asked.

"No," he said, feeling uncertain. He returned the body to the sitting position.

"I'll kill myself."

"That's not fair."

"You think this is fair?" Still face down, she stretched out her arm and pointed toward the boy.

"Why can't you go?"

"I'm grieving. I have to go through a process."

The body slumped over again, dust jetting out of the coat pile in different directions.

"This whole place must be crooked," he said. He chose to leave the body as it was.

"Consider me moved back in. I never should have left in the first place." Her voice sounded like it was coming from a different room. "I hate the way I've treated you," she said. "Sometimes I think that I'm separate from my brain. I do things and I'm not sure why I did them. I'm not always sure who does the deciding."

He stayed silent and stacked logs, heavy and damp, in the pit he'd carved out of the floorboards. He snapped kindling and made a pyramid beneath the logs. He lit the fire and stood there breathing smoke.

"I was hoping we could be a family," she said.

"I know," he told her. Smoke curled in the black part of his eyes.

"I'm serious about killing myself."

"I know," he said.

She flipped back over and brought her knees to her chest. She hugged herself and became a ball.

"You understand what you are asking me to do?"

"I love you," she said. "I've always loved you."

"I won't be the same when I come back."

"I loved you the first moment I saw you. You were with that band of raiders."

"I remember."

"You were dragging bodies to be burned. You gave me clean water. I thought: this man is a protector."

"Who knows what will happen to the boy. There's no guarantee that it'll work. You've heard the stories."

"I can't live like this. Talk to the Surrogate. See what it can do. Please."

The fire hissed. White bubbles, like the saliva of a rabid animal, boiled on the cut edge of a log. Stena lay upright and rigid. He could not look at her. The damp logs refused to fully burn. The fire wavered and let off weak heat.

"I love you too," he said.

Stena smiled.

OUT IN THE city, the snow was so thick Emmons was practically swimming. He followed back roads between the rubble of the old hospital, beside toppled smokestacks, weaving past homes reduced to steel and foundation. The route through the outskirts was impassable. The river had not frozen fully and the bridge was out again. That left the path through the city. He would have to pass the settlement, and possibly engage with and possibly maim or murder at least some of its inhabitants. He brought with him a hunting rifle he believed could still fire and a revolver he was sure could not. He had not seen the locals in years. He had heard the noises they made, but he had not seen them. The noises were difficult to classify. They came to him at night, in half-dreams, bounced off the city's ruins, carried over the empty fields, over the snow. The sound was human—labored and sundry—rising up in unison like a chorus, but it was rigid too, mechanical, the noise an engine might make if it had a mouth and the desire to sing.

Emmons saw the settlement in the distance. The walls were

made of wood; sharpened spears, aimed out at the road, jutted from the stockades. The settlement was built in the carcass of some ruined structure. Smoke rose in black plumes from the settlement's center. The afternoon sky looked flat and hollow. It was a gray piece of paper that could be torn through. The smoke had a flavor that made Emmons's stomach bubble.

He followed the old road through the ruins, through the snow, until he came along a cleared path. He followed the path, climbing over concrete and metal, winding through the burnt out car frames, the piles of frozen garbage. He saw a purple hand in one of the piles, an unblinking eye in another. The ice never melted so the bodies never broke down. He sent his mind searching for memories of the days when bodies were piled up on street corners, when cars were left to rust on highways and sidewalks, but he came back empty. His brain had been strip-mined long ago, those old nightmares replaced with white space.

He arrived outside the settlement where a man in a camouflage jacket sat hunched on a metal folding chair beside the settlement's gate. Across from the gate was a series of wooden sawhorses placed in a line blocking the path forward. The man looked up and gripped the shotgun in his lap. Metal rivers ran in crisscross stitches across his face skin. The rivers were mercury colored, they flowed and rippled as if windblown. The man's eyes were black orbs. His left leg was made of metal.

Emmons wondered if this was a normal way for people to look. He could not remember. He stuck the rifle in the crook of his shoulder and took shuffling steps, walking parallel to the settlement's gate, moving toward the barricade.

"Whoa, whoa, whoa." The man spoke, his words slow and slurred like a drunk's. "Let's de-escalate there, comrade. Let's go back to square one."

"I don't want trouble," Emmons said looking down the barrel of the rifle. It had been so long since he had talked to anyone other than Stena and the boy. "All I want is to pass through."

"Of course. Of course. I get it." The man's teeth were too white, whiter than the snow. The strange lines on his face shimmered and bent when he spoke. Emmons saw the silver lines on the man's neck and hands. "All I need from you is a little information and then boom, that's it, you're on the road again."

Emmons did not speak. He did not lower the gun.

"Like for instance, where are you coming from? Why are you using a path that is not your path? Where is your family? Do they have all of their arms and legs?"

"I come from far away . . . the bridge is out," Emmons said and then tried to remember the other questions. "I have no family."

Behind the man with black eyes, through the slats of the gate, Emmons saw vague shadows moving slowly. He could see a fire. He noticed then that the man's breath was not visible.

"I'm afraid I'm going to need a little more than that. We have certain protocols here. We've realized, after a lot of trial and error, that in order to make any real progress certain sacrifices must be made. We've become a much more open and honest people. We make known our intentions." He straightened his back against the chair. He shifted the shotgun in Emmons's direction.

"I have a home three miles southeast. I live alone. No family."

"That must be hard," the man said, turning his mouth down in a way that struck Emmons as genuine. "Tell me about your plans for the future. Where is it that you are going?"

Emmons could not think of a lie quickly enough so he told the truth. "I'm on a pilgrimage. I need to speak to the Surrogate."

"I like the look of your torso," said the man with black eyes. The mercury rivers twisted subtly.

"What?" said Emmons.

"I didn't say anything," said the man with black eyes.

"I'm not sure that's right."

"A pilgrim? Why didn't you say so before? We make exceptions for the penitent. Believers have the blessing of the Great Body. You may proceed."

The man with black eyes rose from his chair and used his hips to shift the sawhorse blocking the path. He gestured for Emmons to pass.

"Do not be afraid," the man said. "The god we serve is not like those that came before." His metal leg spun and twisted when he stepped. It was made of no metal Emmons had ever seen.

The man saw Emmons starring at the leg. He said: "If your right leg causes you to sin, cut it off and give it to me. I will eat the leg. I will take the leg into myself and give new life to the many-legged."

Emmons did not know how to respond. He walked past the man

and the barricade.

"That's the good word, my man. That's the truth."

"Thank you for your help," Emmons said.

The man smiled his too-white teeth. The silver rivers on his face had stilled. Emmons turned and left him there, but he saw himself go . . . felt his body reflected in the black eyes as he worked his way up the path, toward the factory, toward his blessing . . . growing smaller and smaller in the man's eyes until he crossed the horizon and disappeared into the far-off white.

WHEN EVERYTHING ELSE had crumbled, the factory remained. The walls were black, the windows long gone, but the structure had held, house-sized snowdrifts butting up to the second story, icicles like tree trunks hanging from the eaves. The white print on the brick had been stripped away by wind and time but the outline of the logo remained, the ghost of an animal that no longer existed. He remembered what they called places like this, he couldn't forget the word. Slaughterhouse, he thought and considered for some amount of time the character of that old place-namer. You knew what you were getting, he thought, at the slaughterhouse.

Emmons entered through a hole in the wall. The space smelled like rust and old blood. Crooked shafts of light fell through the broken windows, through the holes in the roof, giving shape to the hooks and chains, the decomposed rubber hoses, the metal grates where the blood had once run off. Emmons remembered an old cathedral he had visited as a child. He remembered the vaulted ceilings and colored glass, the way the air felt inside. His fingers twisted around the wooden barrel of the rifle.

He did not know what he was looking for. He assumed it would be obvious when he found it. Behind his eyes, he saw the boy's body in the snow . . . the green jacket, the wire wrapped around his boot. He descended into the factory. The air grew warm. There were too many rooms.

He walked through thick strips of plastic into a new place. The ceiling here was gone. It was in pieces on the floor. The room was lit up like high noon. Metal troughs lined the walls; the bright sparking across the surface made Emmons squint. In the room's center, he saw a swarm of insects spinning in a dense cloud. Their wings made no noise. They spun and spun around one another, made a loose sphere that breathed like a lung. He crossed a wall of shadow. He moved into the light and saw that the bugs were too large to be bugs. He remembered too that all the bugs in the world were dead. The spinning objects were spherical: little round bulbs. He thought of the black eyes of the man at the barricade. The spheres were silver. They spun so fast as to create the appearance of a solid object. The swarm did not respond to his presence. It continued its indifferent spinning. Moving closer, Emmons was dwarfed by the thing. It was him that was the insect.

Below the swarm, just beside the troughs, was a body, naked and upside down, the face submerged in a pool of water. The body had belonged to a man and it was missing parts of itself, chunks of skin had been carved out, digits removed. He heard Stena's sobbing in the part of his memory responsible for the storage of sound. He waited for an indeterminable amount of time and when the swarm did not respond to his presences, he spoke.

"I don't know what I'm supposed to do here," he said. The swarm swarmed. He felt the air following the spheres in invisible cyclones.

"My son is dead." He tried to trace the swarm's movement with his eyes. Had it changed somehow?

"I want him to be not dead anymore."

Dull lights blinked inside the spheres. They glowed like distant stars. Emmons turned and saw that the body from the floor was standing beside him. It was covered with those same silver scars that he had seen on the barricade guard. The body blinked. Emmons saw that it was missing the left side of its head. The space was filled with silver light. The other gaps in the body, the removed flesh and bone, had been replaced with liquid metal. The thing was made whole. God is a machine, Emmons thought.

"Remove your jacket," the body said. Its voice was wet and empty. "Roll up your sleeve."

Emmons did as he was told. The body was the Surrogate, he realized then. What had he expected? He could not remember.

"Arm," said the body. It gestured with its own rotten limb, raising its right arm straight out from its chest.

Emmons raised his right arm. He looked up at the swarm . . . it was the color of a sunset now, deep red, crossed with streaks of gold. The body opened its mouth in a smile. It had no teeth. There was something silver in its throat.

Below his elbow, Emmons's arm began to burn. He went to touch the burning skin and found that he could not move. He was clinched in a great, unseen embrace. The hairs on his arm cracked and smoldered. An ash-colored smudge formed a ring around his forearm, the sensation becoming unpleasant. The smudge gained depth, moved inward, further into the skin, pressing and pressing until the black gave way to red and the blood fell in twin lines onto the concrete. An invisible blade passed through the arm in halting increments, separating tendons, passing through the bone as if it were made of snow. Emmons saw colors inside himself that he did not know were there. There was more movement beneath the skin than he would have imagined, a great amount of writhing. The limb hung separate from his body, suspended in the air. He had forgotten how to scream. Blood pumped in thick, heartbeat pulses out of the stump until the Surrogate whispered something unintelligible and the wound scabbed over in an instant.

The Surrogate snatched the limb out of the air and lifted it to the swarm. "We appreciate your contribution," it said. "The Great Body grows larger." Swooping down, the red spheres congealed across the severed limb and when they separated, pulled back to the larger mass, the arm was gone.

Emmons inspected the stump. His fingers were far away. His vision was tinted and hazy; the light behind the ceiling had taken on a new aura. It had weight that pushed down. It flattened out the whole world.

The Surrogate approached. It would give him what he needed for the boy to live again. He had made his offering, now came the blessing.

It limped when it walked. The silver lines on its body had turned red, in time with the swarm. It looked as if the body was in the process of separating from itself, as if the light contained within was trying to escape. Now face-to-face, the Surrogate raised a hand, held a finger, pointed up, against its cheek. It pulled at the bottom lid.

It was then that Emmons left himself . . . floated far enough away that he could not hear the sounds that his own mouth made. He drifted off through the ceiling up so high he saw the ruined city covered in white, the concrete skeleton buried beneath. The scab on his stump cracked and began to spurt blood and he found himself back in his body.

The Surrogate pulled down the skin of its face.

"Eye," was all it said.

IT WAS DARK now. Emmons found the path back through the city. His face was wet with blood or tears, he could not tell which. In his jacket pocket was a silver sphere the size of a walnut. Every few steps he would reach into the pocket to make sure the sphere was still there. He wished the eye and arm had been taken from opposite sides. As it was now, he felt unbalanced.

The clouds parted above him. The moonlight made the icicles glow. He thought of water freezing as it dripped, of rivers and lakes solid enough to walk across. He pictured the boy's snow-covered jacket, the barbed wire glinting in the sun. What was he thinking when he froze to death? Emmons wondered. *Please help*, was probably what it was. *If only there was someone who could help.*

After that, the night turned static-colored and liquid. The ground moved beneath his feet. The wind licked the crevice where his eye had been. It felt like being tickled from the inside. He left blotches of red in the snow as he stumbled his way back to the house. Time slithered away.

When he arrived back in his home, having forgotten for a moment what he had gone to do and why he had done it, he found Stena curled up in the coats, her body wrapped around the boy. Emmons tried not to wake her as he pried open the child's mouth and, using two fingers, pressed the silver sphere down his throat until only a dull gray half-moon was visible behind the tongue. When it was done, he let the body fall limp again and fit his own back against the trunk of the dead tree. Stena lay beside him. He put his hand on her shoulder and looked down at the stump where his arm had been. It was purple and bleeding. The side of his skull thumped with pressure; something watery drained down past the corner of his mouth.

The fire pit smoldered. There was very little light left. Stena grumbled, rolled her body off the child and put her head on Emmons's thigh. Deep inside her hair, white specks—tiny creatures—moved across her scalp in jittery, stop-start motion. He felt the warmth of her skin through her clothing. She smelled like a graveyard. He loved her in a way that was painful.

She whispered to him. He could barely hear her.

"I knew you could do it," she said. "The Great Body makes old things new again."

"I don't understand," he said. The room was glowing.

"He's waking up," she said. The room was so bright he couldn't see. "I love you."

He should have never let her go to the schoolhouse. They should have been a family the first time. Now things would be different. He fell asleep with his hands in her hair.

When he awoke the boy was tending the fire. Tiny sparks burst from the embers and gave off smoke. The silver lines on the boy's face burned orange in the firelight. The coat pile was covered in fresh blood. Emmons could only feel half his face. His brain tried to see through his missing eye.

How long had he slept? Months? Years? Had he been resurrected from the dead? Had the earth been renewed?

The sun was up. He saw the light through the boarded-up windows. On the floor behind the boy was a lump of skin and hair and fabric. The hair was coated in dried blood. The skin was bruised and lined with small cuts.

The boy turned from the fire and spoke. "I didn't want to wake you," he said slowly. "But I'm afraid something's not quite right. I don't feel well." Emmons saw the hint of silver in the back of his mouth as he spoke. "Mother doesn't feel well either."

He was too weak to move, so he listened. He noticed that his arm was missing. He felt unable to keep his balance against the tree. His body was slipping and he knew that he would soon fall.

"I need you to do me a favor," the boy said.

FLOW TO THE SEA
Steve Toase

STEVE TOASE lives in Munich, Germany. His work has appeared in *Shimmer, Lackington's, Aurealis, Not One Of Us, Hinnom Magazine, Cabinet des Feés* and *Pantheon Magazine* amongst others. In 2014 *Call Out* (first published in *Innsmouth Magazine*) was reprinted in *The Best Horror Of The Year 6*. From 2014 he worked with Becky Cherriman and Imove on *Haunt*, the Saboteur Award shortlisted project inspired by his own teenage experiences, about Harrogate's haunting presence in the lives of people experiencing homelessness in the town. He also likes old motorbikes and vintage cocktails. You can keep up to date with his work via www.tinyletter.com/stevetoase, facebook.com/stevetoase1, www.stevetoase.wordpress.com, and @stevetoase.

MAJA STEPPED OVER THE LINE OF SALT AROUND THE

Leviathan's corpse. She had just finished laying the circle to keep out Trojans. Her mother had always insisted on establishing a security perimeter before beginning an installation and Maja had kept up the practice. Crystals glittered her hands. She wiped them clean into the sea breeze.

The sperm whale was three days dead and already several holes had opened up around the torso, exposing blubber and ribs beneath. Maja set her programming kit down by the dorsal fin and opened the bag, releasing a hit of wet fur that lingered in the air.

Several areas of skin bulged with the gas build up inside. Ignored, they could corrupt the programming, lead to data loss and ultimately system failure. From her thigh pocket she took out a hollow steel pole, the tip scalpel sharp. Using all her weight she forced the point through the flesh, moving away as the gasses vented from the bloating.

From her programming kit she took out the fox corpse and stroked its fur. Centering the road-kill on a rubber mat to protect it from the sand, she arranged the limbs in the correct configuration. The snails undulated the pelt, giving the impression of breath. A second bag contained rolled algae. She wedged the last strip into the fox's mouth and waited.

The snails sensed the food, opening the fox's jaws, spiraled shells scraping against yellowed teeth. There was nothing for Maja to do but wait.

For the next few hours the snails were concerned with nothing but consumption, replacing food with thick mucus trails, a fine dust of copper visible in the slime. Maja ran a finger along the edge of the circuitry, held it up in the air and watched metal particles glisten in the early evening light. There was beauty here, even amongst so much death.

The snails knew their job. They had been trained to seek out the correct nodes in the rotting meat. Make the necessary connections. It took time. At different moments the chemical composition of their mucus changed, attracting microbes and insects to reroute their networks. She tasted the changes on the air. Subtle shifts in the combination that hinted at thyme, or old brake blocks, mingled with the brackish stench of nearby rock-pools.

After a two-day vigil, barely sleeping, Maja saw the fox's fur flash bright blue for a moment before settling back down to a dirty russet color. She knelt in the sand, peering into the dead creature's eyes, an imprint of the whale's corpse just visible in the milky white pupil. The connections were in place, the network live, the server up and running.

Finishing her cup of lukewarm tea, she walked across to the whale and placed an ear against the flank. The movement was slight, but there. A twitch of electricity along the skeleton as marrow caramelized into high density memory storage.

Satisfied the installation process was underway, she picked up her phone and dialed the client.

THE CARS PULLED up at the limit of the dunes, not risking the shifting beach beyond. Maja looked up from the fox then back down.

Checked the connections were holding, the right parasites gathering along the snail's connections to carry the data, then strode across the sand to meet Mr. Hither.

"Thank you for coming out to see me personally," she said. "I know you're very busy with the wider project at the moment."

He shook her hand and shoved his fingers back into his jacket pocket as if the salt in the air would scar him. He smelt of cheap aftershave and printer toner. She looked at his safety boots, the leather polished to mirrors.

"Is the server online?"

"The program is installing as we speak. It will be another few hours before you can run the cables down to start hosting data. The location is fairly exposed. I would recommend applying a skin coating to preserve the integrity of the storage. A non-invasive surface material won't disturb the internal processes."

On the horizon she saw more suited men, some observing her through blank-lensed binoculars. They always travelled in packs, like cards. She heard the saying in her mother's voice.

"They can come closer," she said, gesturing to the observers. "I know the server is a bit ripe, but they would only be here for moments before boredom and technical language scared them away."

Mr. Hither sighed and ran a gloved hand through his over-perfect hair.

"They have not come to see your handiwork. They have come to recruit you."

She lifted the fox's head to check the installation process. Programming was installed over 56% of the whale's skeleton. Already storage locations were starting to become active.

"Colleagues of yours?"

"Of a sort," he said. "Please, Miss Benfield. This way."

Though they wore the same dark suits as Mr. Hither, the cluster of men were vastly different from her client. They were dressed in sweat and scowls. The reek of damp rooms and questions clung to them like lichen.

"We hear that you are a very gifted programmer, Miss Benfield."

They were interchangeable, but the one who spoke was older, his hands covered in fine white scars.

"Software Engineer is my job title," she said, leaving a gap for him to respond. He stayed silent. "Though the boundaries between the different roles are more fluid these days, Mr. — ?"

"Gunnerside. Mr. Gunnerside. You specialize in bio-servers?"

"My job is to establish the circuitry and install the bio-software which allows animal corpses to be used for the storage of data, yes."

She glanced toward the sea. Without her noticing, the men in suits had circled around to enclose her. Her hand went inside the pouch on her thigh and grasped the drainage bar.

"We have a job for you. A repair job," Gunnerside said.

"A job offer? That's very generous, but I'm fully booked for the next few months. Once I've finished here I have several projects lined up."

"It wasn't an offer."

THEY GAVE HER time to check the installation process, ensure everything was progressing well enough that she could detach the fox corpse.

Opening the door, they waited for her to climb in and then two of the unnamed suits sat either side of her, Gunnerside sliding into the front passenger seat beside the driver.

"What's that smell?" said the suit to her left. Maja opened her bag. The fox's lifeless head flopped backwards.

"That will have to go in the boot," Gunnerside said, pointing to the half-rotten creature. Two maggots fell from its ear. She scooped them up and pressed them down its throat.

"Only if you want to show me your insurance policy to cover the re-acquisition and programming of a new monitoring console."

Several looks went around the car that did not involve her.

"Just keep your bag sealed, and don't let any rot fall onto the upholstery."

"Any rot from this is worth far more than your upholstery."

THIS WASN'T HER first security contract and she had learnt that hidden government installations were either in the middle of the moors or the middle of the woods. This one did not disappoint. They drove for three hours, two of them surrounded by a vast deciduous forest. Maja pictured the different connections. Mycelium spread throughout the thick rich soil. Trees gifting chemical signals to each other through barely touching roots. Vast untapped computing, but they were living systems and forbidden. She sat back and waited for the inevitable barbed wire and guard posts to appear.

They drove through the gate, and a concrete slab of building appeared with no visible entrance. The car paused, engine running while Gunnerside spoke in a language she did not recognize and the wall faded with a gelatinous dissolve. A ramp disappeared into the depths underneath the block of architecture.

THE ROOM REEKED of oil heavy recycled air. Light came from bioluminescent algae behind a thin strip of stained glass running around the walls.

"Please, take a seat," Gunnerside said, pointing to the head of a horseshoe table.

"Do I have a choice?"

"You can stay standing," he said, pulling out the chair.

The wall shimmered and resolved into viscous pixels, shimmered again showing a rotting carcass surrounded by a swirl of waterborne dust.

"A crypto-server?"

The man nodded.

"A bathyal organic crypto knowledge management server, to give it the full correct title."

"What program does it use?"

"Osteopelta."

"Mirabilis?"

"Ceticola."

After reaching under the table, he placed a large box on its surface.

Maja lifted off the lid, the brackish stench cloying in the small room. Fifteen sea snails clung to the Perspex side, cone shaped and unmoving.

"I don't know this OS. I know nothing about the software architecture, and I've never worked with this program. I can't help you."

"Your mother built it."

"My mother has been missing for five years."

"The data storage is deteriorating. We need it stabilizing."

She held her head in her hands.

"What data storage system are you using?"

The man pressed his fingers together and the screen zoomed in.

"Osedax?" Maja said.

Using osedax to manage bone data storage was her mother's signature development. She remembered the boneworms in her laboratory aquaria, their root structures spreading through the host material. Each sector of data stored as a male hidden within the female's harem.

"I'm not my mother," she said, looking toward what she could see of the steel door beyond two more suited men blocking the way.

"Well, you're not a criminal for a start, so you have that in your favor. The data has started to deteriorate and we need an update installing to halt the decay."

"Deteriorate in what way?"

"There is evidence of the information moving into a bacterial mat filing system and we do not have anything in place to recover it. We suspect it's either built in obsolescence or a time bomb hack."

"I don't know this system," she repeated.

"No one does. It's a prototype."

"Then get someone else to repair it for you."

"You might not be your mother, but she did train you. She was very reluctant to do that for anyone else."

"And if I don't agree?"

There was a pause. He pressed his fingers together once more. The screen changed, showing a charge sheet with her name at the top; underneath, written in perfect copperplate, an extensive description of biohacking a live human into a living terminal.

"This never happened," she said, picking up the tank of sea snails and lifting it into the air until bleached algaeic light shone through.

"It has happened somewhere, but it might take months to establish your innocence. Years."

"You're blackmailing me?"

"Persuading, and please put down the operating system. They are valuable enough that depriving you of your life is cheap by comparison."

"I'll need a new monitoring console," she said, opening her bag to stroke the fox fur. "Reynard won't work at such depths. A natural death."

"Natural death?"

"For some reason an anthropogenic death corrupts the ability to hold data. Also there is a moral aspect."

Gunnerside laughed.

"We're far beyond moral aspects here. Anything else?"

"A mammal. The architecture of other classes is not compatible.

Fresh. Within the last twenty-four hours. It can be preserved to bring it to me from the death site. Then I will need time to install the program."

"That will be possible. We'll keep you in accommodation here."

"Keep. Like a pet? Or a prisoner?"

"Like a recruit. Anything else?"

"Where is the server?" she said, taking a seat.

"Not here," the man said, laughing at his own joke.

Maja sighed and pulled the tank of snails toward her once more.

SEA SPRAY COATED Maja's face in chapped skin as she stood at the prow of the research boat. The ocean was rough enough that her stomach did not want to settle, the company in the cabin poor enough that she did not want to go and lie down. The bathypelagic suit under her clothes was already bonding with the keratin in her skin, a process with the sensation of hot wax. She scratched at her arms, but it did nothing to ease the discomfort.

"We'll soon be at the storage site. Are you ready?" Gunnerside lifted her arm and drew back her sleeve, staring at the slowly spreading scaling.

She snatched away from him.

"I'm doing a job for you; I'm not your property."

A smile flickered across his face.

"Make sure you're familiar with the task in hand."

"I'm as familiar as I can be for someone who has never even seen this operating system actually working."

"We won't be able to intervene in any way."

She pulled her sleeve back down.

"You're actually starting to sell this to me."

THE DIVE-MASTER pressed a clump of macro-algae into her hand.

"Am I supposed to smoke it?"

"Shove it into your cheeks. We've tweaked the structure to store and release oxygen over a protracted period. There might be some discomfort as the strands bond with the skin inside your mouth, but it's preferable to the alternative systems."

"The alternative systems?"

He took a diving knife from a sheaf on his ankle.

"The alternative system is that we cut in gills and use an accelerated process of DNA damage to alter your oxygen processing system. This at least is temporary."

She pressed the mass of foliage between her gums and cheek-skin, wincing as strands forced their way into saliva glands.

THE BOAT SHRUGGED the waves above the dive site. Maja stood in the middle of the deck and went through the safety checks. The divemaster helped slide the bag containing the dead seal onto her back.

"Don't think that you can just swim away," Gunnerside said. "The macro-algae won't keep you alive forever."

"That's a reassuring thought," she said, hooking her legs over the railing. "I'll bear that in mind."

The water enclosed her, sweeping over her head. She let herself sink. Watched the ship disappear first, the light go next. Cold seeped through the scales' second skin. Her vision split then settled as the small implants of bioluminescence began to illuminate her descent.

There was no way to communicate with her controllers above and she was grateful for the silence. The chance to concentrate and ready herself for the coming task.

Descent was fast, the weight of her bathypelagic suit dropping her through the mesopelagic to the data storage zone below.

There were predators in the water, but they ignored her, the armored skin she wore masking any scent as she descended. Waves of plankton and fish swarms brushed against her as if she herself was a mammal fall.

The macro-algae tasted bitter against her tongue, and pressed up against the roof of her mouth as it filtered oxygen down her throat.

The whale was vast, a humpback turned belly up by the descent through the water. Most of the skin had been gnawed away by scavengers, leaving the inside exposed. She kicked over to the corpse and peered inside.

The architecture was beautiful, each osedax sector established to be locked away from the next, passing through a series of cryptographed bacterial patches that allowed a unique code to be generated far beyond any encryption Maja had ever seen before. She recognized her mother's handiwork. The delicacy in the location of the data clusters, the specific complexity of the data gateways at the juncture of the bones. Around her marine snow fell, coating her in the decaying white of the dead.

The cause of the data loss was obvious. Near the head of the server a vast bacterial mat had already started to develop, leaching data from the main clusters. All organic servers had a shelf life. Another thing her mother had taught her.

"Always transfer out valuable data before you think you need to, Maja. Don't get caught out."

But this was not natural. It was too early, and the backup systems should have kicked in already.

She laid the seal on a nearby rock and opened its eyes. Already scavengers were latching onto its exposed cold skin. Until she connected to the system there was no way of establishing what the cause of the deterioration was. She felt for the snails under the skin and pressed them forward towards the snout, then laid trails across to the whale.

It took three hours for the connection to go live, then three more for the monitoring device to decode the first level of cryptography. The seal skin flashed blue then settled back. She tilted the head and gazed into the dead eyes, searching for the fault.

There was no fault. There was no error. There was intent and sabotage built into the system. A cluster of osedax set to decay at a faster rate and release enzymes to accelerate the data loss. She rerouted one of the snails to connect directly to the vast bacterial mat. Nothing. The mass of data was so scrambled through the bacteria and had broken down the data into an unreadable mess. The sectors were not just disassociated but fractured and split.

She scraped away at the bacterial mat. The data leached into the mass of cells was unrecoverable, as her mother always intended it to be. Underneath the ulna and radius still clasped together by the silt. She cleared away until the wrist joint, beyond a spread of finger bones half obscured by the wafting fronds of macro algae, torn free of a gasping mouth and held out by a drowning woman as she killed the knowledge she held.

Maja disconnected from the bacterial mat and turned her attention back to the server, knowing what she was going to find. The control cluster was still intact. A small knot of 17 osedax, her mother's favorite prime number, each containing a doomsday program to decay other sectors.

There was no way to save the data. She looked at the cluster as the water swayed the bone worms on their anchor points. The evidence of her mother's intent.

THE SNAIL LAID the circuitry along the top of Maja's mouth and down her throat. She felt the copper draw electricity from her, route down along the mucus. The snail reached her chest and wore through her skin to her ribcage. She screamed, but the algae took her voice.

Lifting the scales around her torso free of her skin, she exposed her ribs with a single cut of her diving knife. She had only moments until the suit spread into place once more. Holding the bone worms in one hand she opened the wound, forced them in and waited.

They spread their roots across her bone, acid breaking down the protein. The data started to transfer into her, shifting across in a series of broken images. Her mother had encoded everything. The threats.

The blackmail. The torture. The designs and the deceit. How to return to the site when the scavengers, both human and not, had moved on. How to recover the data.

There was no need for a server now. For a monitoring device. Maja was the computer. Maja was the program. Maja was the data and the system. Maja was the memory her mother was unable to become and Maja had plenty of time to wait beneath the sea until they forgot. And when they forgot? Maja would reboot and remind them all.

HOUSE OF WAR
Virginie Sélavy

VIRGINIE SÉLAVY is a film scholar, writer, and editor. She is the founder and former editor of *Electric Sheep Magazine* and was co-director of the *Miskatonic Institute of Horror Studies*–London. She has edited *The End: An Electric Sheep Anthology* and contributed a chapter to *Lost Girls: The Phantasmagorical Cinema of Jean Rollin*. She has also written about *Peeping Tom* for the inaugural issue of *Monstrum and Victorian London in Film Locations: Cities of the Imagination*–London. Her work has appeared in publications including *Sight & Sound*, *FilmRage*, *Rolling Stone* (France), and *Cineaste*. She is currently working on a book on Sado-Masochism in 1960s-70s cinema.

THREE MONTHS AGO I WAS AS NORMAL AS ANYBODY. I HAD

a decent job, a nice home, a pretty girlfriend. I liked drinking beer, watching films, and playing video games. "Grow up," my girlfriend would say, as girlfriends do. If only I'd listened . . . to her, and to Jack too. But no, I wouldn't stop, I had to keep going, I had to see for myself. I thought I had it all under control. And now, well . . .

I am writing this because my memory of events is dissipating rapidly, my sense of self dissolving a little more every day. Today I woke up to find that I had forgotten my girlfriend's name. Only an old, dirtied, creased letter addressed to her, dating back five years, which I discovered behind the hall cabinet while looking for lost signs of my past life, resurrected her name. Julie Robinson. Holding the letter like a precious relic, I said it aloud a few times, almost like an incantation. But it did not resonate. It did not conjure up any tender images, any warm feelings, any kind of familiarity. Nothing, as though she were a stranger. And yet, it must have been her name. Judging from the date on the envelope, we lived together for over half a decade. I desperately cling to shreds of the past, hoping that reminding myself of the man I used to be will slow down this frightful deterioration.

Every night the nightmares are becoming sharper, denser, and more real. Every morning, I find it harder to recognize the room around me, the objects surrounding me, the bedside table, the clock, the chair, the wardrobe. They seem contaminated by sinister shadows and metallic glints, their surface tainted by rusty stains, their shapes smeared with a thick, black substance. I dare not leave the bedroom, its familiar, repetitive terrors are all that I can take. Who knows what fresh horrors lie outside the door?

Sometimes my vision swarms with tiny black dots as though the wallpaper pattern was disintegrating around me. Or is it insects buzzing in the air, invasive and belligerent? Perhaps it is only sand in my eyes.

All my strategies are becoming ineffectual. Singing the songs I think I used to like, reciting multiplication tables aloud, going through the alphabet in infinite loops, all to try and keep that monstrosity at bay. But it is becoming stronger all the time. Soon, nothing will block it out. At first I thought I could forget, I hoped time would erode its malignant power. But each passing day has nurtured it and helped it grow, as though it fed on my very resistance. It is there, inside my mind, barely contained, ready to discharge its loathsome pollution at any moment.

I have little time left. The black ooze is gaining ground, the darkness creeping in, gathering around me, corruption eating away at my soul. And the smell, that awful smell . . . I scrub and scrub everything clean, but it will not go away. Is it real or just a sickened echo of that wretched thing? I can no longer be sure. All my certainties have crumbled and soon I won't even know how to tell my tale. I must hurry.

THAT FATEFUL DAY is so crisp in my mind, so acutely, achingly outlined among the opaque, murky muddle of my memories. Everyone in the community was talking about it. A new level of experience, they said. It will blow your mind, they said. There is nothing like it in the world today, they said. So that Friday I joined The House of War. How I wish I hadn't . . . But at the time, it seemed like just another game, nothing more. My best friend Jack had joined, and I enjoyed playing with him. It was as simple as that. I had no idea what lay ahead. How could I have known?

The premise of the game was straightforward, even a little banal. In a vast desert, the United Federation of Allies was fighting the Army of True Faith. In multi-player mode, the game allowed you to play as any of the characters, on either side. I had, rather conservatively, chosen to fight on the side of the UFA, as special agent Ivan Massoud. A Russian-Afghan national, Massoud was an intelligent-looking, dark-skinned, quietly muscular character who spoke French, Russian, Dari, Farsi, and Arabic and was well versed in all types of weaponry and infiltration techniques. Why I chose him, rather than the strong-shouldered, square-jawed, all-hero General Nathaniel Chain, I don't know. I certainly had no desire to be Julian Suzuki, the autistic computer wizard working on countering the ATF in their murderous dark web operations. There was no promise of adventure in that.

On the side of the UFA was also Jane Abdalla, member of the Angels of Death brigade, which was entirely composed of women. Jane's family had been massacred by the ATF when she was just a child. Doe-eyed and cold-hearted, she was an expert in stealthy assassination operations. I hoped I would cross her path.

Always the contrarian, Jack decided to play on the opposite side;

it would raise the stakes, he said. The ATF's commander was the charismatic, almost messianic, Augustus Ibrahim Kanuni, who claimed to descend from a Roman emperor and an Ottoman princess. He was seconded by Wladislaw Patel, a mathematical and strategical genius educated at Harvard, who was also a violin virtuoso. Niels and Mercedes Meyerstein were a couple of scientists rumored to be working on a terrible biological weapon. Any of these characters would have made for a great avatar, but Jack chose instead to play as Said O'Neill, a slender, timid-looking young criminal and self-taught explosive expert who had only recently joined the ATF. I must admit that I was disappointed. In my view, he had picked the weakest character.

An online session had been arranged for that Friday evening. Restive and jittery, I logged on half an hour before the appointed time. Finally the game started, and I suddenly found myself in a foreign land. The desert looked astonishingly real, each infinitesimal grain of sand sharply distinct, the ochre mass tactile, compact and fluid at the same time. You could almost smell the dryness, feel the implacable heat burn your nostrils as you breathed. Standing in the UFA's camp looking at the infinity of dunes, you knew that somewhere out there, hidden among the sprawling alien folds, was the evil heart of the ATF, the fortress of sand where all their dreams of destruction were fomented.

As Special Agent Massoud, I went back into the military compound for the morning briefing. In the UFA's command centre, Lieutenant Abdalla was standing at the back of the room, sheathed in a tight black bodysuit, aware of everyone in the room under her lowered eyelids, her supple, slim body discreetly alert as though ready to pounce. Captain Suzuki was sitting in front of a computer, projecting images and graphics to illustrate General Chain's briefing. A map showed the oil fields controlled by the ATF, their main source of financing. General Chain had sent two agents on a sabotage mission, but they had been caught and executed by the ATF. Lieutenant Abdalla would now take up the mission, renamed Operation Scheherazade. She did not even acknowledge the order, the only sign that she had heard an almost imperceptible tensing of the jaws.

Next, as Captain Suzuki projected the curiously smiling faces of the heinous Niels and Mercedes Meyerstein behind him, General Chain explained my own mission, codenamed Operation Aladdin. I was to befriend Said O'Neill, who, according to our information, was having doubts about the ATF's methods, and infiltrate the organization through this weak link. My mission was to gather intelligence on the biological weapon that was being developed by the Meyersteins. As far as we knew, it was a devastatingly infectious auto-immune disease that caused the body to shut down its essential organs by tricking it into thinking it was fighting a virus. I was elated and congratulated myself on my choice of character: this was a mission that would deliver the thrills and dangers I was craving. And I could not but relish the fortuitous workings of the game that were leading me to become a false friend to an enemy who truly was my friend.

I had been told that I would find Said in a café he often visited in the nearby town, and so I packed a bag and I set out under my assumed identity: I was a French-Tunisian night guard named Omar Breton sympathetic to the ATF but unsure about joining. But whereas I knew Said was played by Jack, Jack did not know that I was Omar. I transformed my appearance by shaving off my hair and putting on glasses and a beard. I appreciated this extra layer of identity confusion. Knowing it was Jack that I was deceiving made it even more exciting.

It was easy to find the café, a dark, dingy little place packed with intense, shifty men. At the back, sitting by himself, smoking mechanically, absorbed in noxious whirls and thoughts, was Said. We struck up a conversation, and as the smoke started to get denser around us and the sky darker outside, we drifted into more intimate, personal revelations, mine all fake, naturally. How odd it was to talk to this smooth-faced young man, knowing that Jack was the puppet master behind him. Said seemed astonishingly naïve and imprudent, confiding to a stranger like me. But I had to remain vigilant. Jack was an experienced player, and this could be some sort of trick. Despite his own faltering conviction, Said agreed to take me to the ATF's headquarters, but not before warning me repeatedly that, once there, it would be impossible for me to leave, should I change my mind.

The session ended, the game would resume the following day. I wished it didn't have to stop, I was impatient to see what would happen next. That night I was visited by Jane Abdalla. She was hovering over me, a black silhouette radiating toxic warmth, holding a knife, the glint in her eyes harder than the blade's. I woke up with a weight on my chest and a sense of dread that I could not shake off.

The ATF's headquarters was a low, black bunker nestled in the sand like a giant beetle. Before we approached the hidden gate, Said asked me again if I was sure I wanted to enter. Again he warned me against it. Turning muddy eyes on me, he said he wished he had never joined. You don't know what they're capable of, he said. You haven't seen, he said . . . His voice trailed off and he looked away. But I would not be so easily thrown off and so we proceeded. Once in front of the bunker, he signaled to a concealed camera and the seemingly monolithic black wall opened to let us in. Inside, a maze of dimly lit arched corridors, grainy and ochre, criss-crossed dizzyingly.

Said led me down a corridor that curled in and out until it unexpectedly emerged into a patio streaked with shimmering rays, despite the absence of windows or skylights. In the middle of the room, surrounded by the obsessive repetition of identical geometric patterns, Augustus Ibrahim Kanuni sat on a carved wooden chair incrusted with mother of pearl, as still as a statue under the unnatural pool of golden light, his eyes closed as though looking inwards. As startling as this sight was, it was not what surprised me the most in the room. At the feet of the sanguinary killer was the last person I expected to see there. Wrapped in opulent, bejeweled, translucent veils, eyes modestly lowered, silent and submissive, was the daunting Jane Abdalla. There were chains on her delicate bare ankles.

Alarmed and flustered, I could not take my eyes off her shackled feet. What did this mean? Had she been caught while attempting to blow up the oil fields? Or was she a traitor to our side, a willing slave to the tenebrous leader of the ATF? At that moment, Kanuni opened his eyes. They were hard and sharp like obsidian, lit from inside by a dark glow. Reeling from their impact, I had to remind myself that I was a highly trained agent and an expert in infiltration. Kanuni's questions were cryptic and oblique, but I must have chosen my answers well because when the interrogation ended I was allowed to stay. But I would have to undergo a trial before I could become a full member of the ATF. I cast a troubled eye on Jane as I departed. Said took me to a bare cell enclosed by sandy walls and locked me in. Kanuni's orders, he said. I sat down on the cold stone floor.

The session ended, leaving me rattled and agitated. I wondered if I had played this right. I got up and started pacing around the room. The game had taken an unpredictable direction. I had not anticipated so much irresolution. Had I really given the right answers to Kanuni? Had I succeeded in infiltrating the ATF's compound, or was I effectively their prisoner? Was Said friend or foe? Was Jane traitor or hero? And what form would my trial take? I could not wait for the game to resume.

At last, morning came and we started again. Said returned to take me out of my cell. Silently he led me down serpentine corridors until we reached a large room partly decked in white, green, and blue tiles, the upper part of the terracotta walls inscribed with mysterious foreign scriptures. As we entered I was immediately aware of Kanuni's pernicious presence, surrounded by his generals, forbidding in their black uniforms. To test my loyalty to the ATF and my determination to join, I was given the task to penetrate the UFA's compound and kill as many allied soldiers as I could without being caught. The number of victims would determine the level of my commitment, and therefore my rank in the ATF.

What a peculiar situation I found myself in. In order to fulfill my mission for the UFA I had to perform what seemed like a reverse mission for the ATF. To loyally carry out the task I was given by my General, I had to treacherously kill my fellow comrades. I had not expected such moral complexity in a war game. "Ultra-realistic," they'd said. I had assumed they meant the violence. As I looked away from Kanuni, I noticed the silhouette in the corner of the room for the first time. Jane, slippery and immaterial, was standing motionlessly, her beauty the only certainty.

My decision was made almost instantly. I had to do whatever it took to succeed in my mission. Said and another ATF soldier had been designated to lead me through "enemy" lines. They were to witness my kills and report back to Kanuni. Soon we were in view of the UFA's barricades. We approached the compound without being seen, climbed up the wall, and jumped down on the other side. A soldier came out of the barracks. I pounced on him from behind and slit his throat without a sound, then dragged his body behind the building. I entered the sanitary block. Two men were showering in the cubicles, naked, exposed, their backs to me. I approached the nearest one and strangled him silently. His body slumped soggily down on the wet tiles. As the other man turned around, I lurched and stabbed him in the stomach. Next to the showers was the infirmary. Furtively, I went in and rapidly unplugged two patients from their life support machines. As the shrill wailing of an alarm began to resonate, I slipped out and found my two companions where I had left them. We climbed back over the wall and scurried away into the desert.

Kanuni was pleased with my performance and I was promptly integrated into his army. An unmitigated success, I believed. This meant I would be able to wander freely around the bunker. All I had to do now was find a way of getting into the Meyersteins' lab. I was moved to a dormitory with the other ATF soldiers. But as I sat down on the bed assigned to me under Said's heavy gaze, I began to feel uneasy. Had I made the right choice in sacrificing comrades for the good of my mission? Where would this path lead to? I wondered what would have happened had I refused to kill my fellow soldiers. This was a truly unusual game. Each session ended not in clear-cut win or fail, but in unredeemed ambivalence. Instead of the usual kinds of gratification, the insidious teasing left me with a growing sense of uneasiness. I was impatient for it to end to find out how I had performed.

That night I slept fitfully, taunted by a succession of indistinct, leaden dreams streaked with confused anguish. Perhaps I could already sense what was about to happen.

The game resumed. All ATF fighters were called for a shooting practice. As we were led through the convoluted corridors down to the range, I saw a dark-haired woman in a white coat open a black door at the end of an arched passage. It had to be Mercedes Meyerstein, I was sure of it. Thrilled by my discovery, I tried to mentally map out the way so I could come back for a clandestine visit later. But first I had to concentrate on the task at hand. We were ordered to shoot five rounds of five. If we failed we would be locked in a cell for as many days as the number of missed shots. I could not afford to waste any time in finding the information on the Meyersteins' virus. Luckily I was a good mark. The tall, sharp-featured ATF fighter who had accompanied me and Said on my trial mission missed six and was led away by guards. Said, unsteady on his feet, his hand trembling between each shot, seemed doomed to fail, and yet improbably hit the target every time. I was next. Tension made my hand seize a little but soon I settled into the task. I hit one target after another, automatically, unthinkingly, until I got them all.

We were then taken to an obstacle course in a simulated forest, next to the shooting range. But as we started jumping over puddles, crawling through pipes and climbing up nets, I realized that Said had vanished. Puzzled by his absence, I completed the course and came first. We were being taken back to the dormitory when Said, haggard, wide-eyed, and moving in an oddly dislocated manner, burst out from a corridor on my left and jerkily yanked me away from the group. "Get out, you've got to get out of here now," he said, the words coming out strangely garbled, his hand spasmodically clawing my arm. "It's me, it's Jack, you must listen, there's no time to waste, you must get out while you can." Suddenly, ATF guards emerged into the corridor and grabbed him roughly. As they dragged him away, he continued to shout, "Get out! Get out now!"

Taken aback, I was led to the dormitory with the others. I didn't know what to think. Why did Jack use his real name? Was it a fault in the software? Was it part of the game? Was he trying to further complicate the friend or foe set-up so I would make a mistake and fail? Or had something really happened? That seemed unlikely. I decided the most reasonable course of action was to ignore his warning and continue. After all, it was only a game. What could happen? And if there was truly something going on, I wanted to know what it was. What an arrogant fool I was. If only I'd listened . . . how I wish I could turn back and take a different path. But it's too late now, all has been warped and soiled and corrupted, only because I have eyes to see.

I cannot recount what happened next without finding myself shaking violently. To deliberately bring to mind what I so desperately try to keep at bay . . . but I must tell my story.

As the guards led Said away and the rest of my group continued towards the dormitory, I slipped off unnoticed in the direction of the mysterious lab. I got lost in the tortuous tangle of corridors, which at times looped on themselves, or stopped abruptly in malicious dead ends. Finally I thought I had found it. At the end of yet another sandy corridor was a black door that looked like the one I had glimpsed earlier. It had to be the Meyersteins' lab. I walked towards it cautiously, a knife in my hand, hoping I would not encounter anyone, ready to act quickly if I did. The door wasn't locked. I slowly pushed it open on to darkness, my heart pounding. An awful noise assailed me, shrill, aggressive, relentless. The room seemed to blur and decay, as though layers of obscurity were being peeled away. Deafened and disorientated I tried to locate the source of this assault, thinking it must be a malfunction. Suddenly, it popped up right in front of me, an ambush. I could not help but see it. It was just there on my screen. Oh how I wish I had looked away. How I wish I could erase it from my mind. Two black figures, masked. Holding a man, tied up at their feet. A third figure, but what was he doing? A large serrated knife in his hand. Why serrated? A pool of thick, dark liquid on the floor. I knew I should look away. But it was too late. I had seen it. The knife hacking crudely through the flesh, the torn shreds of skin, the slashed ligaments hanging out, the blood pulsating out of severed arteries, the strange gurgling sound it made, the neck partly detached, the body quivering uncontrollably, the eyes bulging out wildly, a spark of horrified life still lingering in them. I recoiled and fell backwards, my hand over my own wild eyes, desperately trying to find the blasted control, press stop, make it end, get out, get out, get out, isn't that what Jack had said?

When I looked again at the screen, it was blank, the atrocious vision gone as though it had never existed. I shut my eyes again. I must have lost consciousness. I don't remember going to sleep that night. When I awoke, burdened and breathless, nausea knotting my stomach, I noticed that my girlfriend was gone. When had she left? Was she ever there? I cannot be sure of anything anymore.

Since that moment, I have lived in terrified confinement, afraid of opening my eyes, afraid of closing them too. It had only been a fugitive horror, a brief flicker of hell, but it has remained carved into my mind, branded on my pupils. It is always there in front of me, on waking or in dreaming. The carpet of my bedroom is as cold as stone, the air stale and stifling, but outside can only be more hellish. On the other side of the door may lie renewed reminders, refreshers, reruns, repeats. In any case, I know there is no escape, nowhere that could offer cure or sanctuary. I have been infected and nothing can rid me of this abomination. It lives and grows inside me, eating me up. My thoughts have shrunk around it, leaving nothing but defiled, diseased remains of what I once was.

I wish I could go back and start again.

But I have eyes to see, and I cannot unsee what I have seen.

MUSIC IN THE AGE OF SHEEP

Charles Wilkinson

CHARLES WILKINSON's anthologies of strange tales and weird fiction, *A Twist in the Eye* (2016) and *Splendid in Ash* (2018) appeared from Egaeus Press. A full-length collection of his poetry is forthcoming from Eyewear in 2019 and Eibonvale Press will publish his chapbook of weird stories, *The January Estate*, toward the end of the same year. He has contributed regularly to *Nightscript* and his SF/Fantasy stories have appeared in *Weirdbook* and frequently in *Theaker's Quarterly Fiction*. He lives in Wales, where he is heavily outnumbered by members of the ovine community.

NOT A TREE NOR A BUILDING – AND NOTHING MOVING IN THE

landscape, the sheep having already been moved down into their vast subterranean hangars to avoid the intensity of the midday heat. Athens Tipwarden was early. He parked his vehicle on the banks of the Rea, one of the best preserved rivers in the area for which he was responsible. Private moments of serenity were rare in his job. As he gazed at the undulating grassland, cropped to springy perfection by generations of sheep, and the iron and steel interplay of light on water, he felt privileged. In spite of the risks, he had never regretted relinquishing the opportunity to devote his life to Great Refuse Mound XXXIII, although the Tipwardens were the hereditary overseers.

He looked up towards the heights of the Mouse-Clearing and the heath land beyond. The rising temperature triggered thousands of sprinklers that lay hidden in the earth. Athens saw the precious geometry of water, the intersecting arcs and loops, the subtle darkening of the grass, and in the distance hills glinting as if embedded with silver. He switched on the external sensors and adjusted the pitch and volume until he was surrounded by the gentle lapping of stream over stone, the languorous sigh of the sprinklers. It was comforting to know that even the most seemingly mute blade of grass was emitting its own sound. Such acts of sensuality were still permissible. If a community of Non-Readers, for example, had been under greater than ordinary pressure, they were often referred to an audio-therapy space where soothing sounds, waves breaking on a beach, whale song, or the music of fountains, would be played to them until appropriate levels of happiness were restored. Sometimes the treatment would be complemented by visual imagery: the clamor and violence of a simulated thunderstorm counter-sensitized by scenes of candlelight and flickering fires, the sensation of safety at a time of danger. Readers were not encouraged to attend these auditory feasts. Athens wondered for how much longer they would be permissible even for ordinary members of the public, now that so many members of the Council of Conservatoire were taking literalism seriously. Then there were the Ultra-hummists, those who were not only intent on forbidding all forms of music but also believed that the replication of natural sounds was an affront to Borfamagordia.

Athens reactivated his vehicle and crossed the Rea. It was only a short drive to Mouse-Clearing.

THE VEHICULAR PORT was open when he arrived; clearly the automatic outposts were working once again and had watched him coming up the road. After placing his right hand on the identification pad, he drove straight in and parked by the lift. He had not expected a summons to the Regional Assessment Hub since his appraisal was not due for several months. Conductor Halix was a man who was on good terms with Athens' parents and had encouraged him when, instead of accepting an apprenticeship in waste disposal and recycling, he opted to apply for the arduous five-year course that enabled him to qualify as a Reader-Driver. The door opened and he stepped out onto a landing lit by a combination of artificial and natural light. Although they were deep inside the hill on which it was thought the original Mouse-Clearing had been built, a complex system of shafts, lenses, and mirrors textured the walls with reflected weather. Once again, Athens put his hand on an identification pad and, after the light flashed acceptance, swiped his card on the Secretary. A screen rolled back soundlessly and he stepped into Halix's office.

"Ah, Athens," said a thin man, rising from behind his glittering steel desk, "I'm glad that you were able to come so promptly. Not too many rearrangements to make, I hope?"

"Remarkably few for this time of year, Conductor."

Halix gave a slight wave of his right hand, dispensing with the need for further formalities, and then indicated a seat. He had a full head of soft white hair and lean, creased features.

"I'll get straight to the point. I know that you're very busy. Have you ever heard of time capsules?"

"Aren't they relics of the Later Cow Period?"

"Archaeologists tell us these were metal containers that were not just lost or abandoned. They were deliberately buried by our forebears at some point during the last decades of the Age of the Cow. They were nearly always used to store artifacts and manuscripts chosen as being representative of the small communities that produced them. They are not government records. The people who interred them, not necessarily men and women of great importance in the societies of their time, simply wished some tokens of their ordinary lives to survive."

"This suggests they must have anticipated the Discordance."

"Possibly. Of course, it proved to be nothing like the previous fatuous predictions of the end times, but simply a catastrophe, the inevitable consequence of more than a millennium of self-inflicted wounds. The end of a way of life. Almost the end of all of us."

The Conductor's room was made entirely of materials that reflected light: glass, chrome, aluminum, polished steel, and silver. The designer had ensured there were no straight lines: the walls curved sinuously and even the desk was shaped like an island, its edges smooth and glinting—like tide-washed white sand. As Halix continued to speak, the watery gleam and gloss moved as the light shifted and changed, almost as if it were responding to the fluidity of his voice, expanding, contracting—controlled by the hypnotic rhythms of pause and progression.

Athens thought of the sheep in their hangers, preternaturally pale in the glare of artificial light, moving slowly in impeccably managed acres—chomping the viridian grass.

"The peoples of the Age of the Cow," added the Conductor, "had a view of music that was quite different from ours. For them music needed neither to be for the benefit of society nor in praise of Borfamagordia. A large part of the populace spent their lives intoxicated by vile rhythms. Of course we know the consequences."

"And what is my connection to this?"

The Conductor leaned back in his chair, looked upwards, and pressed his fingers and thumbs together. Some variation in the light was draining the color from the room.

"As a man whose grandfather gave his life in the wars to abolish the saxophone and a Reader-Driver who has done much to suppress the addiction to illicit music prevalent in our remoter territories, you will be aware that your devotion to Borfamagordia is not in doubt."

"Thank you, Conductor."

"Two months ago a time capsule was discovered during an archaeological dig not far from here. Inside, a number of items had been preserved, including some documents and recordings. All of these have now been carefully examined by scientists and historians at the Central Assessment Hub and their findings presented to the Conservatoire. It has been established that you are descended from the man who buried this capsule. Unlike previous objects of this nature, no attempt has been made to reflect the lives of a community or nation. Everything we found was either created by or belonged to this man. This is what will be required of you. You will be given a period of further training and then be asked to go to the Central Assessment Hub to listen to these recordings. The documentation found in the capsule proves they are compositions by one of your ancestors. A Director has been detailed to supervise you. This may take several months, and so I'm afraid that at the end of this week you will have to resign your Driver-Readership. Provisions will, of course, be made for your wife and child."

As ATHENS DROVE away from Mouse-Clearing, he saw the sheep had started to come out of the hangars, the flock leaders moving with uncharacteristic speed, as if enticed by the green spaces opening up before them. Already there was something darker in the blue sky, and they would have, at the most, an hour and half before nightfall. From the crest of the hill he could see the dusky hollows of Digbeth and Deritend and the dull gleam of the Rea.

By the time he reached home, the day had begun to fade to iron-blue dusk, a sliver of soft pink on the horizon. The light in the small watchtower that protruded from the earth was on and a minute later the front field hatch popped open and his son came out to greet him. The boy was wearing the hooped tunic from which he had become inseparable.

"Daddy, you're back."

"And so I am, Little Observant One."

"I'm not Little Observant One," he said with the full scorn of his nine years, and then after some thought: "Well, I'm certainly not little though I might be observant."

As they went down into the main room, Athens saw his life-partner glancing up anxiously at him. It was obvious she'd forgotten he had been called to the Regional Hub. In the last few months, Fern had been more and more wrapped up in their son and the problems he was causing at the Junior Learning Centre.

"This time they want to see both of us," she said.

Athens looked down at his son. His blond hair was disheveled. One eye was slightly brighter than the other, as if he were about to cry down the right side of his face. His left shoe was missing.

"What have been doing, Ash?"

"Playing."

"No, at the Learning Centre."

"I was singing in my own way."

"Again!'

They ate in silence and waited until the boy had gone to bed before discussing his problems. This time he had been singing an unapproved song, possibly he was extemporizing rather than performing forbidden work, while pretending to be a stag, antlering his arms and fingers ostentatiously. He had upset the Monitors by encouraging other children to join in. They had been found in the water area, locked together, chanting and strenuously rutting. At the moment the curriculum consisted of team activities, learning how to employ the voice activated technology they would use throughout their lives and oral world knowledge. At the beginning of the next academic season, however, it would be decided which children would be taught how to read music. But what was important was not simply to have the capacity (nearly every child had this to some degree) to be sufficiently alert to master the required skills swiftly; it was also vital to show mental equanimity, to have a psyche that would not be unbalanced by dangerous knowledge.

Athens sat quietly for a moment, sipping the warm, velvety chocolate. They both found it hard to think of their child growing up as a Non-Reader.

He found Ash lying flat on his bed and staring at the ceiling. He had been crying from both eyes, although the right one was redder than the left. A battered monkey with a disconcertingly steady gaze lay on the floor.

"I'm sorry if you're upset, Ash," he said quietly. "But you must stop being imaginative. It is forbidden to make up these ridiculous songs."

"Why?"

"True music is always in praise of Borfamagordia. The only exceptions are when the sounds created are in some way beneficial to the Humma."

"But I thought that my song was good. Everyone liked it."

"It is for the Controllers of the Conservatoire to decide which songs are permissible. Only after many years of study is it possible for someone to create work that will find a place in the Canon."

His long eye-lashes were thick and wet, his regular features paler than usual, except for a faint flush on his cheekbones. He was a good-looking boy, but what chance did he have of forming a life-partnership if he became a Non-Reader?

"But what's so wrong with making something up?"

"We have been through all of this before. Your mother and I wish you to be richly inventive, capable of contributing useful ideas to the society in which we live. But imagination is uncontrolled invention, either pointless time-wasting, such as claiming, even in jest, to be a stag or a beaver when you are not, or something seemingly wonderful, such as creating one's own unlicensed song, but actually so dangerous, so frightening, that it is impossible to speak of it coolly. The people of the Later Cow Period were the last generations to allow people to make their music freely. They destroyed their governments, their institutions, their countries and most of their populations. That is why there are so few of us: why there are more sheep in the fields than there are people in homes."

"I don't understand," he said a little more loudly, now plaintive.

"At the moment it is not for you even to try to understand. True music is the product of devotion to Borfamagordia, as well as being a branch of higher mathematics. Something in which you are not at present qualified. You do want to train for a Readership, don't you?"

"Of course—and I will. All the Monitors say that I am clever and memorize the parts well."

"Ash, it is not enough for you to be clever; you must also be right-minded."

Defeated, Ash turned onto his side, bringing his knees up towards his chest; the eye that had cried the most faced towards the pillow.

"Please, don't do it again, Ash. You know your mother and I have great affection for you, but you simply must do as you're told. You may be observant and very soon you will no longer be little. Then you will find that to act and speak in the manner to which you have become partial will not be so promptly forgiven."

In spite of himself, he closed the door softly. Fern had tidied up and was watching the tropical fish in the aquarium. Since Fern had given up her job, in order to devote more time to Ash and his problems, she had become increasingly moody. The therapeutic benefits of the aquarium helped her to cope with her son and his idiosyncrasies. Nevertheless, he could see that the complaint from the Learning Centre had distressed her.

"I've spoken to him," Athens said, "and for once I was allowed to have the last word; it is just possible that this time I may have done some good."

"It's been so wearing," she said. Fern's eyes were glazed with tiredness and despair. Not even the fish in their quiet world of slow-moving color could soothe her. "He's singing to himself the whole time in his bedroom. I've tried to get him to sit down with me so that we can practice the Collective Hum. But he just won't concentrate."

"Well, there's nothing more we can do about it tonight. He was very upset, and I think he's finally realized how worried we are. Let's hope so."

He told her he was stepping out and might even check that the refuse containers hadn't been attacked by the magpies again. A minute later he was standing in the cool night air, leaning against the watchtower. In the distance he could see the steady light of his nearest neighbor, a ranger with Drivership status; and far above, the icy scimitar moon and the vast glittering network of the stars. How absurd to think the men of the Age of the Cow had tried to reach them and got no further than placing a few footprints on a piece of rock and photographing a dead planet or two. All while their own people were starving in deserts and murdering each other nightly in the city that lay beneath his feet. What folly!

With Ash's indiscretions weighing heavily on her, it simply hadn't been the moment to tell Fern about his visit to the Regional Assessment Hub and his talk with Halix. Any sort of change worried her, although she might have been proud to hear he could be in line for additional musical training.

As Athens walked towards the refuse containers, he saw a white shape like a cloud hovering in the night. There was little light from the moon and so it was hard to estimate its distance from him or see how far it was above the surface of the earth. But whatever it was continued to move towards the house, although it was not proceeding in a straight line nor at a steady pace, but drifting first one way and then the other, pausing, sometimes for what seemed like half a minute or more, before advancing; in the process it became more solid and less cloud-like, as if it were drawing strength from the night air. Then a thin line, a little more slender than the trunk of a sapling, came from the whiteness above until it touched the ground. As he watched, first another line and then two more emerged and the shape gained definition, seemed composed of pale matted leaves. Just as he had decided that some strange white spinney was sidling towards him, he realized what it was. A sheep must have detached itself from the nearest flock. Perhaps its microchip was out of order and so it was no longer being centrally guided. He saw it had not been sheared recently, so it had evidently been at large for some time. The sheep was now moving towards a small beech tree and had started to eat the topmost leaves. He had heard that the animals from which these sheep were descended had been small, timorous creatures that showed aggression only during the lambing season and then only if they felt that their offspring were threatened. But now Athens was not sure whether the creature would revert to its original nature or act in way that was hard to predict. Should it come into contact with the watchtower, it was capable of uprooting it in an instant. It was possible that if he moved forward the animal would take fright and scamper off in the opposite direction. On the other hand, he did not wish to excite its curiosity. If it had not been linked to the network for more than a month, it would have had time to develop all sorts of behavioral idiosyncrasies. At least it had not noticed him. For the time being it was content to continue munching its way through the foliage of the beech tree, stripping its bark. He could, of course, go immediately back to the house and inform the Regional Animal Watch, but if the sheep destroyed the watchtower he would probably face the embarrassment of having to contact the Hub to ask them to dig both him and his family out.

Before he could make a decision, he noticed the sheep's legs were no longer visible and its fleece was beginning to blur. And then came a few bars of a melody he'd never heard before. He was unable to locate its source or name what instruments were played. Perhaps it was a kind of acoustical mirage caused by strange weather conditions. Soon the sheep was nothing more than mist swimming in darkness. The sounds faded with it. In the moonlight, the bones of the tree were raw-knuckled, arthritic, wounded where teeth had bitten the joints.

WHEN FERN AND he had arrived at the Learning Resource Centre that morning, the screens were flickering into life and a harassed Monitor, a short young woman in a baggy green uniform that must have been made for someone else, was still frantically reprogramming the first activity of the day.

It was some minutes before the Coordinator emerged imperturbably from her office, the well-cut lines of her gown, her recently styled hair and air of calm contrasting with the confusion that surrounded her.

"I'm sorry to bring you in like this, instead of simply making another screen appointment," she said, "but I do feel that there are still some things that are better not discussed remotely."

Athens thanked her and they went back into her office. He glanced at Fern. She was clasping her hands tightly in her lap, as if she were trying to prevent them from springing up and holding her face.

"I'm sorry to have to tell you that there have been concerns about Ash," said the Coordinator, settling herself behind her desk. "The Assessors have examined footage of his group and single-learning behavior and they found that during on-screen time he is not efficiently engaged by the educational process, and has the appearance of withdrawing into the self, while on other occasions he is almost too interested in the material and becomes overexcited. At assemblies he does not always join in with the Collective Hum."

"Yes, we have spoken to him about that," said Athens.

"Last time we screen-conferenced we were all agreed Ash has been very slow to grow out of his imagination. As you are aware, we have been giving him some extra help, but I am afraid he has not responded as well as we would have liked. His use of his spare time has been a cause of concern."

"Yes, I heard about the stag and the song. We've both spoken to him. I'm sure it won't happen again."

"Unfortunately, it's not just that. Did you know he has taken to stoning the magpies by the refuse bins?"

"Oh," said Athens, turning towards Fern, who shook her head. "We're aware that he has no fondness for the birds, but..."

"More than once. He has been repeatedly reminded that all animals are part of Borfamagordia's creation and are to be treated with respect."

Before Athens could reply, The Coordinator peered at her screen. Fern shifted uneasily in her chair, the creaks louder than the audible crack of her finger-joints. Her pale face retreated into the cave of her dry hair.

Athens could hear the lift doors opening in the corridor outside, followed by the babble of children's voices. When The Coordinator looked up, it was the first time since the beginning of the conversation that she had not met his eye.

"It has been determined," she said, "that the best course of action at this stage would be for your son to receive assisted development therapy. There is no doubt what Ash is," she continued, glancing for a moment at Fern before at last turning her level gaze towards Athens. "It is a question of what, with our support, he can become."

"Will this mean he will be away from home?" said Fern.

"Yes, I am afraid it does," she replied, standing up. "Of course, if you have any doubts about what has been decided you may contact the Assessors."

"No, I am sure they know what will be for the best," said Athens as they moved towards the door. He would have to ask Halix what their rights were.

OUTSIDE, THE AIR was already perceptibly warmer. It had been a hot winter, the sky cloudless for weeks now. There were four more months left before they would have to retreat beneath the earth and live like the sheep: machined nights like the gloss of black metal, lime green dawns, and the orange underground sun. There would be a few April dusks to enjoy outside and then on good days maybe an hour or two of evening before the heart of the summer, the air still parched from the burning day, rendering even the nights unbearable. Athens drove his vehicle slowly through the ice avenue and then took the road to the north. It was a journey of about two hours to the Central Assessment Hub; the weather would be cooler there.

He had passed Gravelly Hill and was driving through the flatlands. On either side of him open fields stretching to the horizon, and no trees or hedges—just grass. Some sheep were moving in what he knew must be the distance because they looked small as their ancestors, white scraps in a green immensity under the wide tall sweep of the sky. How many of them would be slaughtered for summer? Athens thought of the echoing underground abattoirs, the sheep coming in innocently from the fields to find the doors to their hangars shut and then something inside them directing them deeper into the earth to die in a white-tiled wilderness, the reek of their blood in the air, the butchery splashed and dribbling on the walls. And after each throat had been impersonally cut by a preset blade, slicing at the same speed and exact angle year upon year, and once the meat had been automatically cut up, packed and sealed, only then would the humans, the Non-Readers in red-stained overalls, come in and set to work on the heads, their hands ravening in the sheep brains for the microchips, every man hungry for them, these tiny pieces of metal still slippery with blood, each to be given in later for a small reward.

Two hours later the flat lands gave way to hills of regimented pine. The verges were lined with gorse and wild flowers whose names Athens did not know. A rabbit skittered across the road and was swallowed up by the undergrowth. Although it was almost noon, he did not stop when he saw the sign for a charging post and an ice avenue. He had enough power to reach his destination and the screen indicated that the vehicle was not overheating.

As he came to the crest of the hill, he looked down at the copses that dotted fields lined with grey walls that dated from the Age of the Cow. He drove down into a valley, past a stream flickering over burnished stone. The road spun out in front him, straightening and then coiling, as if beckoning him deeper into the landscape. And then for a moment the way before him would vanish behind the side of the hill, only to emerge seconds later, teasing him onwards, offering a brief vista of ancient woodland, a blur, soft greens and grey-blues, ambiguous on the horizon. It was these moments, voluptuous with mystery, and a sense of an unnamable presence on the other side of the inscrutable blue sky, that he had come to value above everything. Such times were rare and more often he was at the mercy of palpable dread or a swooning sadness that was halfway between pain and an ache of pleasure. Was it this that his son would inherit from him? The beautiful poisoned richness of the world?

He had just passed a deserted Cow Age village, now little more than a few mounds of moss and ivy, when it happened. Earlier, his sensors had picked up some unfamiliar noises, a dull thud and a sound like a giant coughing. He had seen a few puffs of smoke in the distance that lingered momentarily before being dispersed by the wind. And then, without warning, the dark forest on the left side of the road exploded in a welter of broken branches, rabbits and a black blast of skyward crows. This was followed, almost immediately, by a stupendous ram, its fleece bleeding, and braided with twigs, wreathed in leaves, tattered ferns and splinters of wood. It crashed out onto the road in front of him, its mouth open and foaming, its eyes black and shining with terror—and one broken horn wincing in the sharpened light. At the same time, came the music: a curious melody, with the same clandestine instrumentation he had heard on the previous occasion, that seemed not so much to issue from the creature as to accompany it. He braked in time to avoid it as it thundered across the road. In an instant, it was slipping and tumbling down a steep bank . . . leaving a trial of flattened bushes and crushed saplings in its wake. Then it righted itself with an effort and headed back into the forest from where it had emerged.

Athens opened the communicator and contacted the regional authorities. A recorded message informed him that they were already aware of the problem. Several sheep—they were guarded about the exact number—had lost connection with the network and had now been officially designated "at wild" in the vicinity. Every available ranger had been called in and it was hoped that the outbreak would be brought under control as soon as possible. In the meantime, the Northern Authorities were doing all that they could to minimize the inconvenience to residents and other area-users. Members of the community were instructed not to approach the creatures as they could be dangerous and to report any sightings of unofficial ovine maneuvers at once. Vehicles were advised to proceed with caution. No mention was made of the music. Theological orthodoxy had it that just as light was the gift of Borfamogordia, so all the sound waves that streamed munificently from the first source emitted individual notes on coming into contact with any object, whether animate or not. Most were inaudible to the human ear. Was what he had just heard the essential musical signature of a sheep, the unique harmony implanted in it by Borfamogordia?

As the vehicle wound higher up the hillside, the ancient forest gave way to pine trees and moorland, patched with gorse and heather; in the middle distance, he saw bald mountains, steep gorges, the scurf of exposed limestone, places where man had never lived. If he had not turned the audio-director on, he would certainly have driven straight past the place. Now that he looked carefully he could see a watchtower almost concealed behind a clump of bushes.

ONCE ATHENS HAD put on his gloves, the Director passed the folder. The hall in which they were sitting had been part of a limestone cave. The silver floor undulated almost imperceptibly and the tables and benches appeared to have been made out of frozen water. Their translucent surfaces gleamed while something inside them, the color of liquid steel, flowed upwards from the ground. The only chair, which was occupied by the Director, looked as if it had been hollowed out of an iceberg.

"This is what we have lost," said the Director, as Athens opened the folder.

He turned the antique photographs carefully. The beasts' bodies were almost square and their legs surprisingly slender; the females had great-pimpled half moons swelling from their bellies. Some were white and black, and others the soft brown color of fudge. One animal with horns and broad shoulders was charging a curiously attired individual wearing a strange black hat and carrying a red sheet. But most of them appeared docile, and some of the close-ups showed them staring into the camera with sad brown eyes or with straw or grass sticking out of their mouths. There were shots of them grazing in small fields or sitting together under spreading oak trees, the blue-black bloom of rain clouds above. In one picture they were walking down a high-hedged lane followed by a man in a cap and a small dog with pointed muzzle, a breed that Athens had never seen.

"They gave us meat and milk and cheeses thought to be far superior to that produced by goats or sheep. Their skin was made into leather for boots, shoes, handbags, and coats, a multitude of goods that were used every day. To know all of this, and to have seen these photographs, is to feel their absence in the fields forever." The Director spoke slowly, her hands on the armrests of her enormous chair. "That is why though everyone had heard of them—a whole epoch has been named in their honor—few are permitted to see these pictures or learn what they did for us."

Athens continued to look at the photographs. From the size of the man in the lane he could tell that the cows had been only a fraction of the size of the enormous sheep that occupied the vast, almost treeless plains of the Midlands, the meat basket of the nation. Now that humanity had turned forever away from the cities, allowed the great towers and factories of their ancestors to crumble and be overgrown with grass and weeds, they had made a virtue of their rurality: the sandy, barren pastoralism of the south; the hygienically green spaces of the Midlands, almost empty except for the sheep, the sprinklers, and the pine forests. Only in the north did a little of the landscape of the Age of the Cow survive: a few fields with hedges and dry stone walls; ruined villages; the moors and scarps and fells. And even here mankind was tucked up safely, alive under the earth.

"You have heard, I assume, of our discovery?" She was looking at him with slight amusement. "Nowadays they always neglect to inform me of how much they have imprudently revealed."

She must have been a great age. Her weak grey hair had been cropped close to her skull, her body almost lost in the voluminous blue tunic of a Director. The skin on her face had been pared back to reveal a delicate bone structure. Only her eyes, framed in their sockets as if they were the most important part of her, looked enormous, still vital.

"Yes, a capsule . . . containing documents and some recordings."

"That is correct. It is the recordings. They consist of some songs and what was customarily called a symphony. You will not have encountered anything like them before and will need a period of guidance. The musical language of the Later Cow period does not differ greatly in its harmonic structures. The real problem lies in the mode of expression. For them music was not necessarily in praise of Borfamagordia; it was a form of individual expression, unlicensed and licentious. I see that during the time when you were being prepared for your Readership you studied the counterpoint used during the Early Sheep Period."

"Yes, in my final year."

"Well you will now find that your work will at last have some practical application."

THE DAY AFTER he had finished listening to the symphony for the first time he received a message informing him Conductor Halix was visiting and wished to see him. He found the old man in a small room with a curved ceiling. All the walls and the floor had the smooth gloss of the interior of a seashell.

"It is kind of you to seek me out," said Athens, as they shook hands.

"I have, as it happens, other business here." Halix grimaced as he sat down. "A long journey and one that was not without incident.

Indeed, I must count myself lucky to be breathing."

"Why? What happened?"

"The vehicle in which I was traveling was narrowly missed by an artillery barrage. We appear to be at war."

"War? But war is obsolete. There are only breaches of security."

"When do persistent breaches of security amount to war? It is an interesting point and I shall put it to the Security Committee this afternoon. But I can see from the astonishment on your face you are not up to date with events."

"I have no access to the news. My days are devoted to the music of the Later Cow Period."

"Then you will not be aware that an entire flock, one that was pastured some way to the north of the Midlands, has gone off-network. Nothing like this has ever happened before, or at least, not on this scale. We have been forced to requisition cannons and other weapons from the Museum of War. It took well over a week to create supplies of ammunition and in the meantime these creatures have been leveling anything that lies in their path."

"And we are blowing them to pieces with artillery."

"That is what we are trying to do. At the moment those men operating our armaments appear to be strangers to the arts of accuracy. But these are not matters for this afternoon. I'm afraid, Athens, that I have some unwelcome news for you. Fern has not been well. Her medical advisors and her legal officers have persuaded her to ask for a formal dissolution of your life partnership."

"But surely that's not possible. We have a son."

"Ash is now officially under the guardianship of the Warden of the Institute for Moral Development."

"And so I have no legal remedies whatsoever?"

"You do have the right to appeal against the dissolution of your life partnership. But in the circumstances I would advise you against that course. Read this." He nodded in the direction of the document.

Athens picked it up and thumbed through it. Ash was not even mentioned. What he had heard, but could not bring himself to believe was this: every year a number of children were denied the opportunity to train for a Readership, not for the reason that they lacked the capacity to do so, in many cases they were amongst the most able of their generation, but because in some way, which was hinted at but never precisely explained, they were inherently unsuitable. It was implied their abilities were such that they would never be able to settle in a community of Non-Readers; their presence would be a torment to other more tractable inmates, a cause of anxiety and disruption. These children were removed from their parents and their Learning Centers and never heard of again.

AS SOON AS he came into the room he knew the Director had read what he'd written. She was not looking at him, though her right hand was spread out on top of his treatise, as if she meant to keep it from flying away of its own volition.

"I've read this," she said, still not meeting his eye. "What we were hoping for was a cultural analysis, an insight into what it was in these people that caused them to run amok, to externalize their imaginations and burn themselves up in wars. But this," she said, tapping her forefinger on the frontispiece, "is more in the nature of an appreciation, is it not?"

"I think that what I was attempting was a response..."

"Response!" And for the first time that morning she looked at him. There was loathing in her eyes. It was as if he'd dredged up his vilest emotions from the bowels of the unconscious and smeared them over her face. "Why should a society that gave free rein to the worst wars in the history of the world be afforded the dignity of a response?"

He was being assessed. Had they already found what they were looking for in him? Some clue—the genetic code for the musical imagination, perhaps—something that might help them to breed people like Ash and himself out of their society. Make the country safe for thin-blooded people, living for most of the year huddled under the ground. They would, he knew, dispose of him politely and without pain or the agony of forewarning. He would be buried in some quiet place deep in the forest. And Ash? Was he already dead or still the subject of a few last experiments to test the limits of his singularity?

AFTER HIS SUPERVISION with the Director, Athens obtained permission to spend an hour outside. For a moment, he was tempted to run off into the forest and hide in the hollow trunk of a tree. He would be content with a diet of nuts and berries, a bed of dried ferns and arched roots for windows. There would be a river at the bottom of the valley, and he would drink in the dark with the night animals. Now he knew what music was. This cadence, this joy, the melodies bubbling within him, the rhythms diving and coming up for air, the ecstatic arpeggios, the heart's lilt, the sigh in the bar, the sob of grief, the sea-quest of the imagination.

He heard it coming over the hill before he saw it. At first he thought it must be some kind of outlandish god or a demon conjured from the air. A deep whirr that was not like anything he had heard before. And suddenly it was above him: an inexplicable underbelly of green and brown, a long tapering tail, a great curved eye of glass the size of a window; its wings were a blur above its enormous head. It was only when it circled the Hub and then hovered for an instant that the memory of a half-forgotten visit in his childhood to the Museum of the Air surfaced and he realized what it was: a helicopter!

Since the aeronautical extravagances of the Age of the Sheep had damaged the fabric of the air, all forms of air travel were illegal under international law. The Master Controllers were in breach of an agreement that was fundamental to the survival of the planet. The helicopter moved off in the direction of the Midlands and a few minutes later Athens saw white smoke rising beyond the forest.

That night as he lay in bed not sleeping, he tried to recall the first incident in Ash's short life that should have warned him. The infants were being instructed in the basic sounds of the Collective Hum. Every morning before the beginning of the teaching day the children would be assembled and asked to hum, softly at first and then more loudly, but always harmoniously, so as to form a continuous soothing wave of sound. After a time individual notes vanished into the harmonic structure of which one was a part. And standing in rows, it would be as if the very boundaries of one's body were dissolving in a bath of communal contentment. At times of anxiety, sorrow, or distress men and women would congregate in their central concourses and recreate once again the Collective Hum, the warmth that had embraced them in their childhood. But Ash would always hum too shrilly, too fast, too low, or too rhythmically. His hearing and his sense of pitch were tested and found to be normal. There was, it seemed, no explanation, except there was something in him that would not sink, something forever buoyant, bobbing on the ocean of sound.

AENVALIT
Farah Rose Smith

FARAH ROSE SMITH is a writer, musician, and photographer whose work often focuses on the Gothic, Decadent, and Surreal. She authored *Anonyma*, *The Almanac of Dust*, *Eviscerator*, and numerous short stories in horror and speculative anthologies. She is the founder and editor of *Mantid*, an anthology series promoting women and diverse writers in Weird Fiction, as well as the Community Outreach Director for Necronomicon Providence. She lives in Queens, NY with her partner.

ALL OF LOVE AND GOODNESS HAS BEEN EATEN BY THE

grey. A shadow dives down to the mountaintop—a sky worm of the lightest hue—orange tongue touching the highest peak, then rising again into the frozen aether, pulled by the chain of the sky council. There is no escape from the grey planet. All of dread and gloom lives across this landscape, every eye partially blind—drawn shut against the color and vibrancy of half-forgotten life.

Images decorate the inner eye at times of unrest. There she lies for a while, in a sleepless cradle. Silver light glistens over her, thick hair flowing wild and supreme. The days sink into her chest, like death. Palladia, the Serrammes of Tavoria.[1] Palladia, the crystal of Acuben.[2] This is her namesake. Years from now, in times of despair, she will imagine herself as the deity, wandering in the waking world.

Cold rays beam down over her shoulders, the palest of greys. Years pass on, all the same. When she looks through days-without-light, she holds the egg of the Nabryd-keind,[3] painting oil over the shell to reveal an interior city. It is the only place to see color on this cold, grey planet. With forehead pressed to the surface, she wishes to be caught in this egg of life. *They must not know I have so many*

---

[1] The original incarnation of a deity-like entity in the known universe, Serrammes being the highest title in the hierarchy of Tavoria, a system of quartz planets in a planetary system far from the milky way. Palladia is one of the eight gamemakers and the nemesis of Pseussor.

[2] A term of endearment awarded to her by another gamemaker and her clandestine suitor, Baeldall.

[3] Nabryd-keind is a species of bird-monstrosity from the planet Direforge. They can range from the size of a dog to a large bear, and are identifiable by their long, sword-like beaks and enormous crystalline plumage with iridescent hues of lavender, red, or turquoise. They are uniquely vulnerable to dust-infections.

here, she thinks, eyes drifting to the stolen tome on her bed, then to the closed cupboard. A shrine to cities in color, somewhere else in the universe.

"You eat nothing and insult me again, aenvalit,"[4] says Ivora, a seeth ilf.

Palladia's head is bowed, features dimmed by a sheath of gauze, silent rage obscured by youthful persuasions of the eyes and mouth. Pain and horror burst forth from the creature, bleak in its observations. Thrice in life its pallid form melts into an eel-like organ, which slithers to the nearest sea to absorb enough salt for the next phase of life. Each incarnation becoming more freckled, paler, cruel. An elvish monstrosity from Baeldall's[5] planet. Their sharp ears fold back like limb-plant, sharpening their hearing ... it listens to Palladia when she is sleeping, when she is not sleeping ...

"I am not hungry," Palladia answers, setting her mangled utensils back on the table.

The surface is buried in tired fruit and solemn, undercooked meats. Palladia sits between Krasa and Zadir. More watchers from the outer worlds. The Uldreds grab her wrists, forcing her hands against her plate. She grabs a long bean in one hand, a reedfruit in the other. They force her hands to her mouth. She eats. They laugh.

---

[4] *Invalid*, or *broken-one* in ilf-speak.

[5] Baeldall, Lord of Teranjis, Hand-Bearer of the Cell, High Warden of Candewog, one of the eight gamemakers.

She remembers tales of earth, of those called men. Of her color being drained, pulled from her flesh by orange tubes, let out as steam of every color into the abysmal emptiness, sipped by the worm. Though as it is in the taking of a most precious element, all that was gentle and beautiful was not entirely lost.

Elephantine faces, black teeth, body of man and beetle. Glowing green hooves, double-jointed legs, black robes, and red eyes. The Uldreds from the black moon of Ulldythaer.[6] These secret emissaries of Bezel[7] listen to the Scaerullian[8] choirs at night, hymns to their life-God, Pseussor. The White Thantis of Ulldythaer.[9] Palladia thanks the stars that they are not the flying-kind. She had imagined such in her nightmares—their speechless curled tongues, black baleen teeth snarling in hunger beyond a procession of red clouds.

"What of the activity in town?" it asks, feigning interest.

"Groggins were found with golden scarves."

"And what became of them?"

"They were burned."

"The scarves or the Groggins?"

"All."

---

[6] A planet of black deserts, ancient black trees, a red sky, and strange whistling screams of invisible creatures who thrive on the chemicals in the upper atmosphere. Here resides Pseussor and her council.

[7] The personification of evil in folklore and reality as defined by the *Scaeraulldythareum*. A Cembraselik (sentient-gas) entity visible to organic life as black fog.

[8] Scaerullism is a fringe religion based on obscure teachings in the *Scaeraulldythareum*.

[9] One of the eight gamemakers, a Thantisaur, which is a giant mantis-like creature the size of a mammoth. They are hyper-intelligent and often amalgams, capable of transfiguring into other species. Pseussor lives on Ulldythaer.

The ilf will not meet Palladia's eyes. The yellow hue takes far too much salt to ingest visually. As she swallows the rancid meal, Palladia recalls a single planet, Hathisua—a cold, metal world decorated in ice beyond the black planet. She had seen her pale city in the first egg, collected from the byrd-beast on high, in *his* chamber. It is in this way that she holds on to hope of a return to her life in infancy. With *memory*.

"Should you not eat, and continue, you will be brought to the Grand Overseer,[10]" declares the ilf, long fingers grazing the rotten meat on its plate. It does not know of the nights she spends beneath his sheets of silk, explosions of dread-passion filling her up with cosmically dark juice. The Overseer is indifferent to the ilf's complaints, should Palladia remain wide and at rest within its chamber. Only there can she retrieve the eggs. Only there grows a chance of going home.

I am the aenvalit. I am a watched girl.

DREAMLIKE SPIRITS GATHER around the window, a sudden blueness shattering the evening light. Palladia hums to herself—songs of strangers in golden cities, springtime laments, and colored clothing. Tonight is not for the gathering of eggs, but for a visit with a friend. In the early morning, Palladia must harvest grey-worm for the ilf—leaving seldom few hours to share the warmth of company. It is her only manner of avoidance from the devilsome deeds of night. Deep

---

[10] A political and judicial figure on the grey planet.

in the woods, beyond the grey lake. She is both girl and woman, curious and wise. Palladia crosses her feet on the cobblestone floor, eyes gazing up to the great alien-creature, expectancy blooming as it does when in wait for a story.

"What is this?" she asks, lifting the oblong purple fruit from a glass.

"Proof that life does indeed return from the grey." He smiles, turning towards her.

"Have you an egg for me this evening, Palladia?" he asks.

"Have you another story, Ciiricet?"

"I tire tonight, regrettably."

Palladia bows her head and places the egg between his enormous outstretched fingers without complaint.

"Have you been found out by the byrd, dear girl?"

"It can't hear. It doesn't know of the taking."

"Good."

The byrd of the Nabryd-keind sleeps in the chamber of the Grand Overseer. It is his prize—an avian monstrosity with phenomenal crystal plumage. A gift from the dreaded Tyrant-Councilor on the green planet, Direforge.[11]

She will not tell Ciiricet of the byrd's whereabouts, or her acts of despair. What she told herself she must do, to live as herself someday.

"Precious objects, these," he whispers, rubbing a claw against the shell. Ciiricet pulls a thread from the floating egg, cerulean and frail.

---

[11] A planet of opulent rainforests and millions of diverse and undocumented species.

"So unlike the first, isn't it? From the pale city."

Ciiricet, a strange arctoidea with eel-like protuberances, pulls the thread through a long black needle. He wanders to a corner of the hut lit by grey candlelight. There stands a mannequin in the shape of Palladia, an opulent dress of extraordinary color wrapped around it. The fabric is immaculate, the product of generations of sewing. Palladia watches as he pulls the new thread into the hem of the interior skirt, knowing she is not the first to bring him the eggs.

"How much more is there to be done?" she asks politely.

"One more thread, here . . . " He points to a golden fabric flower above the chest, not yet sewn to the bodice.

A somber tolling rings out from the inner city tower. *His* tower. Palladia jumps, anxiety brewing. Her eyes turn to a casket filled with shattered egg shells—the dead remnants of the interior cities. She is eternally nervous at being found out as orchestrating something beyond the grey.

"I have fallen in love with these cities," she says, "but none so much as home."

Ciiricet puts down the needle, a haze of deep thought obscuring his features.

"What do you remember of home, Palladia?"

"Nothing. Only the egg, and knowing I have been there."

The bell tolls again in a darker hue of sound.

"I have to be back for the harvest."

Ciiricet pats her on the shoulder. He steps out of the corner, head bowed. She pauses, horror filling up her chest, mind swimming with the memory of the old tale.

"Why are we imprisoned here?"

"Because of Pseussor." The tolling grows more ominous. Palladia runs to the door, into the darkness.

"Avre tenesh, Palladashka,"[12] he says.

"WOOSH NYTHITIS OOSH ool dook thear."[13]

The seeth ilf and Uldreds bow to the cosmic deep, grey skin pulsing with the threat of encroaching weather. At the foot of the black gate, their gaunt hands hold the weight of troubled dreams.

"Our graves will be set low on the planet of death," spits Ivora, cruel eyes searching for salt to lick up from the grey dirt. The Uldreds' eyes gleam soul-death in disguise. "Soon Krespel will infiltrate this system with his kind."

"We will not speak of Councilor Krespel,[14] ever," answers the lesser-twin, with a sweep of his gnarled hand.

"Yurrod has long been at law with these worlds, but never so violently as with the Councilor himself. There is no risk from his kind worth attention." The other twin brushes away dirt between them, laying down burned artifacts—pages of books and organic remnants. The ilf sniffs disapprovingly.

---

[12] *All hail Palladia.*

[13] The White Mantid of Ulldythaer, as said in moontongue, also known as dreadtongue, the language of the Uldreds. It has come to be a statement of allegiance to Pseussor, Ulldythaer, and the Thantisaurian cause.

[14] A much-respected though even more feared former politician and commander of the Yurrodisian army. A reptilian humanoid from the planet Yurrod, who now resides on Direforge in a palace filled with hunting treasures.

"And what word might there be from the Thantisaurs?[15]

"Pseussor has come to believe that for the very first time, the Palladian Triumvirate[16] have been born in the same galaxy. And are the same age."

The Uldreds bow their heads, acknowledging a travesty of prophecy they dare not name.

"And where is our aged-Palladia on this night?"

DARK TRUMPETS SOUND beyond the lake. The dark gloom of night lingers on. The moon, like a rock in a tidal pool, ebbs erratically through the frozen aether. Palladia walks past the frozen lake, unable to bring herself to look for the floating spirit. The chains rattle in the distance as loudly as if she were holding them against her skin. Palladia marks the sadness of the floating creature in her heart, but it does not stir. It has no stomach for exterior energy, standing as sentinel over the mysterious frozen corpse beneath the field of ice. Many a time she has passed by this place, without knowledge of the scene at hand. Only quiet rumblings from the ilf about eternal damnation in ice for a known betrayer of the Thantisaurian council.[17] Overwhelmed by déjà vu, Palladia hears gliding

---

[15] Mantid-like monstrosities with extreme intellectual faculties and transfigurative abilities. There are only thirteen left alive.

[16] The original incarnation of Palladia was murdered and their soul was split into three entities, scattered across the universe so that they could never assimilate into one being again. The Triumvirate refers to these eternally reincarnating sister-souls, which Pseussor makes every effort to kill, confine, and monitor.

[17] A council consisting of the last remaining Thantisaurs, which advises the Uldred army, leads their society, and monitors the Palladian Triumvirate.

movement beside her.

"Where do you go, Palladashka?" Black breath hits her cheek, a sudden touch from the Overseer.

"Home, sir." His strange grey-blue head and enormous black eyes are almost visible beneath the cloak of a thousand hues.

"Come with me."

"It is the worm harvest. I would not be chastised by Ivora."

"Nothing bad will happen, dear thing," he says, wrapping his long arm around her torso, pulling her towards the phantom coach—a machinery of science and magic, as all things are in the uncharted worlds—a metal and hideously ornamental ground-ship, hovering over the ice by the electromagnetic power of green-mist.

THE LIGHT IN the tower dwindles, a dull lavender. A luxury for the Overseer, only. The ceiling is a vast sky-map in motion—an ocean of stars—showing the known and unknown passageways for every species in the sector. The grey planet is inaccessible . . . inescapable. Palladia wonders why he may chart such things, if no one leaves, and no one goes.

His body hovers over her, heavy and wicked. She keeps her eyes on the byrd cage.

"Your darksome suffering pains me," he says, removing himself from her. He absconds to another room for a moment, allowing Palladia to stand, to wash. She limps to the iron bars of the byrd's cage. It sleeps some great distance within the wall, in shadow. She has never seen the wytch-byrd of the Nabryd-keind. Only summoned its eggs with the curious contraption she built at home, from the remnants of her father's artifacts.

She uses the moment of solitude to summon the egg with the device, hiding the latter in her hair and the former beneath the bed. The Overseer returns, hands wrapping around her shoulders.

"The poor bird, it decays," he says. "Infertility, says the doctor." He turns Palladia around, lifting her chin up.

"Are you fascinated by the byrd?" he asks. She nods reluctantly.

"Wombs so grave must be drawn to each other."

Hatred fills her up. With unmistaken force, Palladia stares into the Overseer. He kisses her violently. As his hand slides again towards her most intimate parts, she unfolds the egg contraption hidden in her hair and stabs him, grey blood spilling over her face, his weight collapsing before her into mist. The wytch-byrd screams, awakened by the horror, turning the room into a kaleidoscope of vibrations and yellow static. Palladia closes her eyes, balancing herself against the onslaught. She grabs the egg, wrapping it in the silk bed sheets, running from the room as the shadow of the enormous creature gnaws at the failing cage bars. A ripple flows through the overhead skychart—an earthquake beneath waves of light.

This is the last egg, she thinks.

PALLADIA RESTS ON her bed, undiscovered by the watchers of other worlds. She reaches for the borrowed tome, Ciiricet's mangled copy of the *Scaeraulldythareum*.[18] Tired fingers flip past hand-scribbled prose. She has read very little, unable to understand the long passages of dreadtongue and the other unsavory languages it is written in, only reading the story of her namesake. An *aenvalit* would rather marvel at illustrations in color. Such books are forbidden on these worlds. She wears grey clothes. Eats grey food. All is grey here. That is the *law*. Under the icy aether, all that is vibrant is a harbinger of death.

Palladia falls asleep briefly, tired by the onslaught of fear. She awakens with a piercing unease. Glancing towards the fireplace, she sees the ilf, eyes cloudy in its growing blindness. It feeds pages of the *Scaerulldythareum* to the limp fire.

"No!"

Palladia stands and collapses, the heaviness of a seeth ilf poison—sleep-steam—infecting her nostrils. The ilf stands over her.

"You have read *Palladae Pseussora*,[19] yes?" Palladia stares, caught at last in the honesty of her predicament.

"You know of the Palladian Triumvirate?" The ilf asks in its croaking voice, eyes clouding over heavily in the blindness of intense observation.

Palladia whispers, "Yes."

---

[18] An undateable tome that serves as a makeshift almanac to the early universe, filled with planetary science, folklore, and historical events. The book itself, written by an unknown hand with profound insight into the machinations of the universe, is a neutral, indifferent piece, but has sparked everything from casual interest to deep madness in humans to profoundly dangerous religious movements in exospecies.

[19] An epic poem in the *Scaeraulldythareum* that illustrates and describes the origins of the feud between Pseussor and Palladia.

The ilf hits her in the face. Pink blood pours down Palladia's nose. The ilf is overcome by contemplation and leaves the room, locking the door behind it as Palladia slips into steam-intoxication.

Aenvalit
  aenvalid
    Ae
        ae
      aenvalid
              Invalid

PALLADIA IS RUNNING, running far. The skin of her feet break open over thorn-weeds, worm-teeth, and fallen branches. The evening is deceased. Small stars sparkle against her, rising up like high-tide. Screeches follow her sharp gestures of purpose through the wood. She reaches Ciiricet's hut, covered in the pink blood of her ancestors, shriveled pages in hand, with the silk-wrapped egg.

Ciiricet turns to see her in such a state, but does not fret. There is an awareness of all that comes at a point of fateful unveiling. Palladia extends her hand to his. He takes it and guides her to her shadow-form—a version of herself in clay, decorated with the miraculous colors of a homeworld free of the deep-freeze of Pseussor's damnation.

"Do you want to be as you once were, Palladia?" he asks gently.

"No," she says. "I want to be as I am."

Ciiricet removes a gold brush from his satchel as she holds the last egg out to him. He dips the bristles in a cup of oil and glides the brush over the shell to reveal a shocking citadel of the most absurd, ebullient kind. Sharp, cloud-lit towers, orange and pink, yellow and sapphire. Palladia is filled with a strong sensation of *knowing*.

Ciiricet holds three fingers to the crystalline shell and pulls a single orange thread from the interior.

"Was the pale city not my own?" she asks, remembering her sense of affinity with the delicate citadel of the first egg. "The original?"

"Have you not read *Palladae Pseussora*?" he says, pointing to the shriveled pages of the *Scaeraulldythareum* in her pocket.

"I have."

The needle, newly joined with the last thread, travels through the bodice of the alien garment, painting the fabric rose with joyful character.

"Then you know, dear Palladia. They have all been your home."

He begins to remove the dress from the form. As he peels away each layer of fabric, Palladia feels a wave of life flow through her. He holds out the dress to her. She takes it.

"This hue of blue is rather familiar," she says, gliding her fingers across the first fabric layer of the skirt.

"Perhaps you have been out by the lake and gazed beneath the surface?"

Glass breaks.

Palladia is soaked in pink mist, teeth, remnants of skin. Ciiricet is dead, the remnants of his flesh dangling from the light fixtures overhead. The chanting of Scaerullian hymns sounds from the exterior surroundings. The screech of the ilf at the depths of rage. They are here.

PALLADIA RUNS IN the night, tearing her clothes away, the greyness of her flesh glowing beneath the moonlight. She slips the dress over her head, blue, orange, gold fabric gliding across her warmly. She reaches the glacial lake. Pressing one foot against the ice, then the other, gliding with intention, she moves towards the floating spirit and the imprisoned corpse. Water puddles into footprints. The ice is melting beneath her steps, beneath the dress. Palladia reaches them, the great black chain rocking pendulously from its point of eruption in the ice to the ankle of the floating soul. Palladia kneels over the buried thing, hands pressed to the ground, water gathering around her fingers, a hue of sapphire becoming clearer, more vibrant in the melting. The eyes of the Uldreds glow in the distant fog. They are coming.

Palladia presses her body against the ice, fabric swimming around her in an unusual gale, gliding against the legs of the floating spirit, whose eyes stir with the sadness of waiting, waiting.

The Uldred forms grow greater in the distance. Palladia can feel a sliver of fabric encased in the ice at the tip of her fingers. She presses her palm to the sliver, and a great crack sounds beneath her.

All motion is upward. The two beings before her merge in a mystical confusion. Palladia is caressed in sapphire gauze, purple hues, rays of silver and white. She sees the immersion of soul and corpse, an evaporation of chains into black bugs. She begins to rise into the sky, wrists held by the rising being.

The sky worm roars. The flight of the spirit is graceful, but not quick. The great beast swallows them up and, no longer bound to council hands by the great chain, glides through the icy barrier between ground and sky, into the great black cosmos beyond worlds.

I am myself, she thinks, the warmth of saliva running across her body as she is held in wait within the mouth beside a familiar spirit, above a prison of grey, the light of another world's sun growing brighter as she is transported to cities-in-color.

I am as I have always been.

THE TRANSPORTED
Jeffrey Thomas

JEFFREY THOMAS is an American author of weird fiction, the creator of the acclaimed milieu Punktown. Books in the Punktown universe include the short story collections *Punktown*, *Voices From Punktown*, *Punktown: Shades of Grey* (with his brother Scott Thomas), *Ghosts of Punktown*, and the shared world anthology *Transmissions from Punktown*. Novels in that setting include *Deadstock*, *Blue War*, *Monstrocity*, *Health Agent*, *Everybody Scream!*, and *Red Cells*. Miskatonic River Press/Chronicle City have released a Punktown RPG for the Call of Cthulhu system. His other books include the short story collections *The Endless Fall*, *Haunted Worlds*, and *Thirteen Specimens*, and the novels *Boneland*, *Subject 11*, and *Letters From Hades*. Thomas lives in Massachusetts.

MALO L'ORANGE SLEPT ON HIS SOFA, BECAUSE HE HAD

turned his apartment's one bedroom into his lab. The narrow sofa was enough for just him, since Ete-tomi had left him at the end of summer.

He woke, expelled a long sigh as if exhaling intoxicating smoke he'd been holding in his lungs all while he slept, rose from the sofa, padded barefoot to the kitchen section of the central area that served as living room and kitchen both, with just a short length of low partition to pretend it was a separation. He poked a button to summon coffee. His mug had a logo on it, a gold seal enclosing the letters PTC, for the Paxton Teleportation Center. He and all his coworkers had received this mug as a Christmas present one year, but he no longer worked there as of last spring. Laid off after six blasting years; replaced by a robot, no doubt. A company could utilize 50% automatonic workers, no more, but his union had finally lost its long struggle to resist that percentage. He had quickly exhausted his severance package and had only a few weeks of unemployment insurance left to him, then no source of income. No *legitimate* source of income.

Coffee mug in hand, wearing his pajama outfit of T-shirt (again, featuring a fading PTC logo) and boxer shorts, his dark hair an unruly mop, Malo went to the bedroom, poked another button, and a door that sealed off its bottled odor hissed aside. He stepped into his lab, sealed the door again after him.

The room's smell filled him; hard to describe, but smoky, rather like incense, not unpleasant but overwhelming. The background headache he'd awakened with immediately spiked to the level of conscious awareness, as did an accompanying swell of nausea. Yet he was used to these things; they were a normal aspect of his corporeal existence.

It was murky in here, and not just because he had sealed the room's two windows against letting in sun and city light, and letting out smell. He kept artificial lighting to a minimum because his growths favored darkness. Wearing a protective mask at the time, before installing his lab equipment he had sprayed the walls and ceiling with a solution that as it dried puffed up into a yellowish, porous insulation foam that looked like a fungus, or diseased flesh. It both contained scent and muffled the humming sound of the Pipe, lest those in neighboring flats complain of either. The foam made the ceiling lower, made the room seem more intimate, like a kind of womb.

Against one wall was a comp desk that Malo had found on the sidewalk outside his apartment building with the hand-printed sign FREE taped to it. Ete-tomi had helped him carry it to the lift and down the corridor to their flat. Before Ete-tomi had departed, the desk had resided in the living room. That had been before the lab. Now, most of his lab's most critical equipment rested atop the desk's various shelves.

He went to this gear, passed his free hand over a sensor, and a row of holographic monitors blinked into existence—glowing red in the gloom. Below the monitors: virtual dials and keys. He checked some numbers, compared them to a virtual chart of specs he kept for reference, made some delicate adjustments to two of those dials. The Pipe's temperature was to go up one degree, and its steady vibration—which was responsible for the room's audible hum—came down a single notch. Satisfied, he brushed his hand over the sensor again and the red-glowing displays were gone. He sipped his coffee and turned to face the Pipe.

He had set the Pipe in the center of the room, wedged it vertically between floor and ceiling (into the foam of which it disappeared). It was of black metal, thick like a tree trunk. He'd had it modified for him by a friend, from a piece of scrap they'd salvaged from a junkyard heaped with old hovercars and robots. His friend, Zed—who had also helped him bring the Pipe here and secure it in place—had cut six openings into the Pipe, running up its length like the finger holes in a flute. Zed had welded little metal cups into these holes, affixed a cable to the back of each cup, threaded these cables down through the Pipe, and run the bundle of these six cables across the floor and up into a mechanism that rested on one of the shelves of the desk Malo had found.

Malo stepped up to the Pipe, close enough that the carefully regulated heat of its metal could be felt on his skin . . . just as its deep, familiar hum resonated in his teeth and bones. Both the temperature and the deeply ringing vibration were critical components, among others, in the flourishing of the growths nestled into the Pipe. So many factors . . .

Malo had paid Zed—a former coworker who had retained his job as an engineer at PTC (lucky bastard)—with a pound of good quality seaweed for his assistance. Malo had his connections. Friends came in handy, though he kept friend and connection alike at arm's length. Friends and connections could turn, especially if they fell on hard times (as he was about to do), or if the forcers leaned on them.

Four days ago Malo had pushed a gob of reddish-purple flesh into four of the six holes in the vibrating Pipe—it was all he had enough material for. He'd measured and formed these little blobs between his palms, as if shaping hamburger meat, and they had been of approximately the same size . . . so it was always perplexing when some took and others didn't. Was it subtle inconsistencies, fluctuations in the signals conveyed into the metal cups that held them? Factors beyond his anticipation or evaluation.

Only two of the latest gobs had proved viable. The two bad lumps of matter added their decaying stench to the faint mist that hung in the air from the nurturing process—given off by the hollows in the Pipe—like the taint of a decomposing body that funeral incense sought to mask.

He bent to see that in the lowest of the six holes in the Pipe, the clot of flesh there had turned black, had partially liquefied, and glowed with a kind of superimposed, bluish and fluttering static. "Blast," Malo muttered. He set his coffee down atop a cart on wheels that stood nearby, holding a few additional components of equipment. He donned protective gloves, picked up a plastic container, and scooped the failed blob out of its recess into the container. He'd soon take it back to his kitchen and dump it into the trash zapper.

Likewise, the gob in the second-to-top hole in the Pipe had

failed, though it was only beginning to go black and that weird aura of flickering blue static was more subdued. Still, he scooped this mass of cells into the container atop the other, then set it onto the mobile cart. After both masses were removed from the Pipe's charged recesses, the static was immediately extinguished, though they then began to smoke. Even before going into the trash zapper, they were ceasing to exist.

Thankfully, the two remaining masses seated in their sockets were doing well. One of them, burgundy and glossy, had sprouted four little nubs since last he'd checked; and better, the other's nubs had lengthened into little tapered points.

"Hey," Malo said, reaching out a gloved finger and gently stroking the latter mass's smoothening surface between those tapered extrusions. He smiled, like a proud father given a look at the scan of his partner's growing fetus.

It was like some living residue of Ete-tomi, though of course it wasn't. And anyway, an Usumil of Ete-tomi's sex was not capable of giving birth.

THERE WERE ALL types of sentient beings who had settled in the city called Punktown, so there were all types of ways to get there. The Earthers themselves, who had overlaid their colony (originally called Paxton) upon the much smaller city belonging to the indigenous Choom, had first come to this world Oasis in ships, via artificial wormholes called jump chutes—before long-range teleportation eventually replaced that. The beetle-like race called the

Coleopteroids had helped the Earth Colonies to develop that teleportation technology, though as extradimensional beings the Coleopteroids themselves traveled from one plane of existence to another by means of a vehicle called a tran, which moved along a complex, overlapping series of tracks in certain geometric patterns, at certain speeds, depending on which dimension they intended to end up in.

The Usumil race, fairly new immigrants to Punktown, were—like the Coleopteroids—adamant about utilizing their own technology, their own particular method of transportation when it came to teleporting to the planet Oasis. On their end, their memories were recorded and then their bodies were essentially disintegrated, destroyed, upon transmission. On the receiving end, at the Paxton Teleportation Center, waited receptacles filled with reddish-purple blobs of undifferentiated cells that had been grown in nutrient solution, on site, for this purpose, and weighed out in advance in accordance with the precise mass of the individual in transit. The transmitted "soul," as the Usumil thought of it, of each individual was received into one of these waiting masses of cells. Really, this consisted of introducing the genetic code of the transported individual into one such mass of clay, which would then metamorphose into a perfect facsimile of the teleported individual . . . in a process that generally took only about a week. Late in the process, when a brain had developed sufficiently to receive them, the stored memories were introduced.

Malo considered the Usumil method to be more akin to cloning, but Ete-tomi had argued that this was not a doubling. Nothing was left back home. It was more a rebirth.

The Usumil were a striking race; Malo had been attracted to Ete-tomi immediately when he'd first encountered them, back when he'd still been working at PTC and Ete-tomi had just recently arrived. He'd met Ete-tomi when they were seated at a table in a cafeteria off the Usumil recovery room; Ete-tomi was to be released into Punktown the next day. He'd been struck by their beauty. Seven feet tall, with glossy burgundy skin, long-limbed and with an unearthly grace, the hairless head remarkably human-looking but for the black parrot-like beak in place of nose and mouth.

He'd asked if he might join them, had introduced himself as Malo L'Orange, a tech at PTC, and he found that Ete-tomi liked coffee, too. The two had chatted throughout his lunch break, and during that time he had learned that Ete-tomi was a "Mixer." The Usumil had three biological sexes. "Senders" passed spermatozoa to the "Mixers"—as their kind was called, in translation—in whom an egg was then fertilized. Through a second act of intercourse, this egg was then passed on to a third sex, called a "Garden," in which the fetus was grown and from whence it was born.

Depending on the particular nation of Usumil, however, for reasons Malo didn't entirely grasp, the Mixer race might be deemed inferior . . . a mere connective tissue between Sender and Garden, and thus in such tribes the Mixers were often relegated to servitude. Ete-tomi had confided to their sympathetic and increasingly disgusted human listener that a Mixer's fate was frequently a miserable one.

"Punktown's a dangerous place," Malo had told Ete-tomi in the cafeteria that day. "We import crime from every populated planet—as if your situation isn't bad enough already. If you ever need a helping hand, in any way, please don't hesitate to contact me." And Ete-tomi had accepted his contact info, transferred from his wrist comp to the brand new wristband the Usumil wore.

It had only been two weeks later that Ete-tomi had contacted him. Already mistreated, exploited—sexually and otherwise—in the home they shared with their new Sender and Garden spouses, whom they had never met before coming to Punktown.

Malo had gone to meet Ete-tomi at a coffee shop, and then brought them and their one suitcase to his apartment . . . back before the bedroom had become a lab.

MALO AWOKE FACE down on the carpet of the central area that served him both as living room and kitchen. He pushed himself up a little, groaning, just enough to see the pump-action shotgun lying nearby like a lover he'd picked up in a bar the night before. It was loaded with crystal shot; he kept it nearby whenever he had someone over to receive some of the substances he either arranged to have on hand, or created himself in his lab.

"Never do your stuff yourself," someone—numerous someones—had advised him in the past.

Yeah . . . right . . . okay.

He rolled onto his back, moaned at the effort, stared up at the ceiling, fighting the urge to vomit. His skull felt pinned to the floor with lengths of rebar through his eyes. Why had he got the shotgun out last night? He vaguely recalled listening to music (some rousing Del Kahn tunes), pretending the shotgun was a guitar, dancing wildly, finally yelling lyrics that devolved into mindless swears. Then he'd fallen to the floor; he could almost recall the impact before blacking out. He reached to a sore cheekbone, then sat up, realized he was naked. He hadn't slept naked since Ete-tomi.

He got to his feet, stooped and dragged the shotgun to him and picked it up, dropped it on the sofa for now. Went naked to punch up a coffee.

Taking a first tentative sip, he let his gaze slide to the sealed door of his lab.

His friend inside the Paxton Teleportation Center, Zed, had helped him acquire much of the equipment he had in there, had smuggled it out for him component by component, a little bit at a time, via the shipping docks. After all, Zed's cousin was in security; Zed had helped his cousin get that job. Zed had not only assisted a great deal in getting Malo's lab set up after his termination from PTC—Zed was also the one who occasionally smuggled out for him raw chunks of the undifferentiated cells that the Usumil cultivated (on the Punktown end) to receive the memories and genetic blueprints transmitted into them whenever an Usumil teleported to the planet Oasis.

Malo went to the door, opened it, stepped into his lab, holding his breath reflexively against that first onslaught of strange air, only letting it in slowly. The faint mist even stung his eyes a tiny bit, as always. In the center of it all: that black pole, the Pipe, like the last pillar supporting his collapsing life.

"God damn," he hissed, looking into one of the two occupied holes. "Blasting god *damn* it."

You could never predict; it had seemed to be doing well. And yet, the red-purple blob that had started becoming smooth, rather than meatball rough—that had begun sprouting nubs like little organic receptors to receive the charge transmitted via cable into its metal cup—lay blackening in its socket in the Pipe, its flesh overlaid with a caul of static, like a ghost version of itself.

Into the plastic trash container Malo roughly scraped it.

Ah, but the last viable mass of cells. At least—so far—he still had this one.

He didn't want to wait any longer. Though it wasn't fully ripe, he was afraid if he waited too long this fruit would rot on the vine, too. The process was too delicate, too unpredictable, too full of vagaries. Yes, he preferred night for this. Yes, his head still blazed with pain from the purple vortex he had snorted last night, and the anodyne gas he'd sprayed down his throat until the metal bulb had run empty. But, when might Zed again be able to bring more of this matter to him? Purple vortex, seaweed, anodyne gas . . . none of them were the same.

Malo inserted his right hand into a purple glove, reached into the socket in the Pipe, and scooped the muscle-colored blob into his hand. He carried it out, brought it to his mouth, and bit into it like an apple before he could stop himself from doing so.

To his mind, this was the best way to do this, if one was to do this. Not that many did. This was a rare privilege, like some sacred act.

The tapered nubs had elongated even more—had grown a joint or two, in fact. He felt the rudimentary limbs beat weakly at his cheeks as his teeth punched through. A clear pink fluid burst down Malo's chin, down his bare chest. A pop of fluid into his mouth. And then . . .

Flash.

Purple.

A luminous purple sky, and filling much of this ultraviolet sky: three darker purple moons hanging so low that the largest of the plum-colored spheres seemed ready to come to rest on the horizon. Malo had never been there, bodily, but he knew where he was in essence. (Where his *soul* had gone, if he might believe in a soul as they did.) This was the world of the Usumil people.

The world Ete-tomi had come here from.

Oh my God, Malo thought . . . look. *Look.*

Standing there naked in his former bedroom, immersed in the incense-scented mist given off by the Pipe, still holding the dripping ball of cells with its dying limbs stirring the air in its final convulsions, he stared toward the horizon of another world and saw silhouetted against the purple sky several towering black forms, like too-thin giant spiders with too few limbs, looming as tall as Punktown skyscrapers. Here and there they were beaded with gems of red light. They were a kind of animal, not necessarily aggressive but best avoided if possible. Ete-tomi had described them to him, but this was his first time actually witnessing them. *Oh!* He hoped one of them would stride over here, closer! His lover had told him the things were so beautiful! If you looked deeply into one of their nodes of red light, Ete-tomi had said ...

"Uhhh," he heard his own voice, *his own blasting, disruptive voice*, moan in a combination of ecstasy and drunken discomfort. And then he toppled back, like a felled tree, and two worlds went entirely black.

ETE-TOMI WOULD GET irritated at him when he'd slip and refer to them as "she" or "her," though they hadn't minded him calling them "sweetie" or "honey" or "baby." That is, until toward the end, in late summer—after having lived with him, having sheltered with him from their people's persecutions, since spring. Malo had been laid off from his job at PTC only days after Ete-tomi had moved in with him. He'd begun gassing more, smoking more ... though he hadn't begun with the purple vortex. Or, of course, the other.

"Drunk!" the Usumil Mixer would snap at him. Watching him, always *watching* him these days, with accumulating disapproval.

"I wasn't drinking," he'd slur, weaving. He'd been spending time with friends more and more, Zed and old school chums, meeting at bars and such ... but he needed them! He needed them as customers to supplement the meager unemployment insurance payments he was receiving. Didn't Ete-tomi see that? He was trying to *care* for them!

"Whatever ... gassing ... it's the same."

"Honey..."

"Don't call me that," Ete-tomi would say.

He would then go to the much taller being, would reach out to burgundy flesh that in preparation for Ete-tomi's marriage had been covered in a web of metallic gold tattoos, patterns that designated the Mixer's gender. Reaching to caress that glittering lace. And more and more often, his lover would withdraw from his touch.

"I'm just a novelty to you, aren't I?" they would accuse him, sounding hurt and self-conscious. "An exotic fuck."

"No. *No!*" he'd protest. And finally, always, he'd blurt, "I love you!"

"*Love*," Ete-tomi would repeat, with tears rising to their human-like eyes. "It's a trick ... the instinct to procreate. But you can't procreate with me, can you? Love is all just an *illusion!*"

"Illusion is an illusion," Malo would slur.

"What does that even mean?" Ete-tomi would murmur, their tears now liberated, dribbling down their gold-tattooed burgundy cheeks. "Blasting addict."

Ete-tomi had escaped. Escaped their tribe. Escaped *him*. Out there now in Punktown, somewhere. And him, alone, in here.

ZED SAVED THE day. Today he'd brought a new batch of Usumil cell matter; a good-sized tub of it, too. In his lab, Malo set this tub aside on a small table, and at the same table dumped a batch of gel caps from a capsule-filling machine into a plastic bag. He turned and held this bag out to the man who had come here with Zed today, a friend Zed knew from somewhere. This man, whom Zed had introduced as Cantu, was a mutant: his head was topped by a crown of large yellowish nodules or tumors, which, ringed as they were by his curly black hair, looked like various-sized eggs in a nest. After pocketing the bag and thanking Malo, this Cantu person sniffed at the air and then gestured at the black metal pole.

"Hey, man, you grow stuff in that pipe? I heard of stuff like that."

Malo said, "I'm an experimenter," and then shrugged.

"Mad scientist," Zed joked. "So hey, you gonna give me a few of those poppers or what, Cantu?"

"Oh yeah." Cantu chuckled. "Forgot." He dug the baggie of gel caps out of the pocket of his cloned-leather jacket again.

"Forgot, my *assss*."

Cantu handed Zed three of the capsules, then smiled at Malo again. "You ought to sell me some of your experiments sometime, man. I'm always looking for that *more* thing, you know?"

"Aren't we all," Malo said.

OH, BUT THIS batch was good. So, could his success rate have something to do with the age of the material Zed brought him, rather than something he was getting wrong in his lab? Whatever the case, all six of the lumps he had fitted into the Pipe a few days back were coming along beautifully. Smoothing out, the starts of four nubs. No blackening, no overlay of static.

Malo locked up, left his apartment building, walked to a nearby coffee shop—one in the JavaJunky chain—the very one where Etetomi had met him that time after they had fled their abusive spouses.

They had come here together, again, numerous times while Ete-tomi had lived with him. But he hadn't come here alone, since . . . it had been too painful to contemplate. It had felt *wrong* to sit at one of its tables alone. And yet, today here he was, almost masochistically.

It was nearing winter now, so he was drinking a Christmas-themed latte. Ha . . . he thought of his Pipe, back in his flat, as a perverse Christmas tree. Full of presents waiting to be opened one by one. Or, an advent calendar of unearthly delights.

Outside the coffee shop's window loomed Punktown, soaring ominously taller than he could see from here, like a tsunami wave of impossible height that had solidified just before it could come crashing down on him and all the puny vehicles and pedestrians swarming in its shadows. He watched a hovertrain glide along its elevated repulsor track, which passed right into the body of one of the skyscrapers, to emerge somewhere beyond. He watched a holographic banner, in the form of a huge Chinese dragon, with ad copy worked into its undulating body, swoop down and pass low above the hovercars before floating upward and away again. He watched a pair of lovers stroll past right outside the window, two young Choom holding hands, carrying shopping bags, and he activated his wrist comp and called Ete-tomi. Again. They didn't answer, so he bent low over the device and recorded a message.

"Yeah, it's me. Look . . . can we just have coffee sometime? Just talk a little? I only want to know if you're okay. You know, if . . . if it's going to be possible for you to divorce your two spouses. I hope so. I hope to God you haven't gone back with them, especially against your will. I don't blame you if you'd rather be with your own kind, but if so, I hope it's with one of the other tribes . . . the ones that don't see you Mixers as inferior."

He sighed. He looked around him to see if anyone would notice, and pulled a cool metal bulb of anodyne gas out of his coat pocket. He didn't pop its tab just yet, though . . . he wouldn't want Ete-tomi to hear that.

"I worry about you. I know you don't believe this, but I love you . . . I still love you. And I miss you so terribly much."

He sent the message. Now he broke the gas bulb's seal with a satisfying snap.

In furtive sprays, he emptied the entire bulb in the coffee shop, but took the remainder of his coffee back to his apartment. Along his unsteady walk, he decided that he would take the first of the new batch of growths tonight. Again, it might be premature, but once more he reasoned with himself that it was wise to do so before his luck might change, before the things went rotten. One made their own luck, didn't they? Good and bad.

THIS BATCH OF growths was doing so well—had grown so much, and so quickly—that Malo felt uncomfortable about biting straight into one of them, as strangely satisfying as that was. Somehow— though his crop had not transmitted any specific genetic blueprints, of any particular Usumil individual—he could see the starts of heads on them, despite these lacking developed features.

He wondered: *would* they develop features, if he let things go much further? If he removed them from their limiting sockets in the Pipe, for instance, found more spacious containers he could run a stimulating charge into?

Might he grow them, or at least one of them, to adulthood?

The thought repulsed him more than it piqued his curiosity. He elbowed the weird fantasy aside, went to the Pipe and with gloved hands removed the best developed of the growths, which could no longer be called a "gob" or "blob" or "lump." He carried it to the table that held the capsule-filling machine, and lay it down on a bath towel he had folded there.

Malo had occasionally, experimentally, shot himself with the drugs called "fish" and "snakebite" while in college, had even tried mainlining "gold-dust" and purple vortex instead of just snorting them as he did now, but he'd never done any of those substances enough to get hooked. (Especially fish, which could lead to dramatic physiological changes, and not for the better.) Shooting up was not the way he liked to do things. But his crop here . . . what they did for him . . . it was a whole other matter. And he still had old syringes in his possession.

His left hand holding the growth down on the towel, with his right hand Malo pushed the tip of the syringe into the smooth roundness between the thing's four rudimentary limbs. These stubs instantly went into a kind of spasm, twitching . . . one might say kicking. One appendage struck feebly, accidentally of course, against his left wrist. He drew back on the cheap syringe's plunger, filling its barrel with pinkish fluid.

Drained, the thing stopped twitching its limbs. When he pulled the syringe from it, the mass went completely still, and dark tendrils of smoke began curling from it. He flipped the towel over the mess. He'd dump it into the kitchen trash zapper later.

Right there in the middle of his cave-like lab, standing near the mist-emitting Pipe, he tied a bit of surgical tubing around his left arm, then cleaned the syringe's tip with a sterilized wipe. He squeezed his fist several times to pump up his veins, positioned the needle's point over one of these vessels with the beveled opening facing upward. He pressed the metal through his skin with an unheard snap. Depressed the plunger a little, then pulled back on it to see a bit of blood enter the barrel; in this way he knew he was planted in the vein correctly.

Using his teeth, Malo released the tube around his arm, slowly pressed down on the plunger and sent the entire contents of the syringe into his body—into the complex, intimate pathways of his inner microcosm.

Flash.

Purple.

And now *he* was the one injected—into an alien macrocosm.

The trio of dark purple moons—small, medium, and very large—were almost full and dominated the ultraviolet sky. Standing there naked on a flat plain that stretched off toward the horizon of low mountains, Malo could discern areas on the largest of the great spheres wherein delicate traceries sparkled like thin veins of silver. He didn't know if these were geological formations or moon installations of the Usumil people . . . of whom, from where he stood at least, he saw no structure or sign of presence.

But then, peripherally, he did. He sensed a tall figure to his right, turned and saw an Usumil standing beside him, only a few steps away. They were also naked, and from their unique genitals, and also from the gold tattoos woven across their burgundy flesh, he could tell they were a Mixer. And when they spoke, he knew it was Ete-tomi.

His lover was not looking at him, instead gazing off across the plain, toward three towering black forms, like greatly elongated colossal spiders but with fewer limbs, looming tall as Punktown skyscrapers. They were nearer to Malo's position than they had been the last time he'd come here, so that he could better make out the brilliant red jewels of light that marked the multiple joints of legs almost too thin to see.

In profile, Ete-tomi said to him in his tongue, "What do you think you're doing here? Looking for me?"

Malo's eyes filled up. "I guess I am. But I never dared dream I'd actually find you."

"You haven't," Ete-tomi said coldly. "I'm not here. You're just dreaming."

With his tears liberated down his face, he gave a quivering smile and said, "You forget: illusion is an illusion."

MALO HAD TAKEN a shunt line to meet with one of his repeat customers, a Tikkihotto who lived in the neighborhood called Willow Tree, and had sold him a bag of seaweed. With some of the money received, Malo treated himself to a lunch of Vietnamese food at a restaurant called Pho Paxton. He wasn't in bad spirits on his return ride to his neighborhood. His flourishing crop awaited him; he'd inject another of them tonight. He contemplated whether to sell the juice from two or three of them. It was a rare elixir, would fetch a good price—all the more money with which to pay Zed to acquire more material, hopefully as fresh as this batch had been. Still, he hated to part with any of it.

When he let himself into his apartment, he knew right away something was amiss.

The air smelled. The scent was hard to describe but it was smoky, rather like incense, not unpleasant but overwhelming. There was the subtlest mist in the air, just enough to make things look a little faded. Creeping forward, setting down a bag of *banh mi* sandwiches on the kitchen table, he looked toward his former bedroom and saw that its door had been slid wide open.

The landlord, perhaps, come for a surprise inspection . . . maybe in response to complaints from a neighbor about the smell, the Pipe's hum, or his loud music and gassed-up singing/yelling the other night?

He didn't think so. From under his sofa, he slid out his pump-action shotgun. He crept onward, toward the open doorway of his lab.

"Man, we really don't have time for this," he heard a familiar voice hiss. "It can't wait? It can't wait, huh?"

"You just box up the rest," said a voice that was also familiar, but less so.

Malo had reached the threshold, his heart a trip-hammer pounding his interior into a new shape. "Hey!" he barked, the butt of the shotgun braced against his shoulder.

Both men whipped their heads around. One stood at the table that held the capsule-filling machine. Malo recognized him as the mutant Cantu, with that cluster of nodules growing up from his skull. On the table lay one of Malo's growths, wisps of smoke twisting from it. Just now inserted into Cantu's arm was one of Malo's syringes, still filled as yet with pinkish fluid.

The other man was Zed, who stood at the Pipe. When he turned, he had another of the growths cupped in his hands, and had been about to lower it into a plastic container at his feet.

"Oh, hey, brother!" Zed said, erupting into a too-huge smile. "Hey, hey ... easy, there. We knew you'd be home soon—sorry we let ourselves in! We're going to pay you for these, okay? My buddy Cantu wants to buy them all off you ... right, man?"

But Malo flicked his eyes back to Cantu to see that the mutant had let go of the syringe, though it still dangled from his arm, and was reaching around to the rear of his waistband. The purpose of the movement was unmistakable. Malo shifted his shotgun's barrel from Zed to Cantu just as the latter's pistol began to swing into view.

Malo was jolted by the recoil and, enclosed as the blast was in this insulated room, his hearing was instantly and painfully exchanged for a ringing near-silence. Most of the crystal shot caught Cantu in the right shoulder, shattering into jagged shrapnel against bone, all but tearing his arm away. The impact spun the mutant around and he fell onto his front, shrieking.

Malo cut his eyes back toward Zed, began to flick the shotgun toward him too, at the same time that he noticed Zed had let go of the growth—had simply let the precious thing drop to the hard floor—and had pulled his own handgun, a ray-blaster that Malo knew his friend always carried. After all, this was Punktown.

Both men fired at the same time.

Zed was slammed back against the Pipe. It held. He didn't. Malo had got him better than he had Cantu: the 00 crystal shot struck his former coworker right in the mouth, turning his lower face into a raw red chaos, like the unformed Usumil cell matter. The eight projectiles had exploded into smaller crystal missiles against his jaw and cervical spine. With eyes bulging as if in disbelief at his own death, Zed slid down the pole to the floor, propped in a sitting position.

Zed had got off just one shot on his blaster, a bright red ray-bolt that had streaked between the two men. Malo looked down at himself to see a perfectly round hole, deep as forever, burned into his left breast. He swore the bolt must have gone through his heart (could Zed have been that accurate without having time to aim, or was it just a lucky shot?), the wound cauterizing itself along the way. He couldn't see if the beam had exited out his back or not, but it felt like it.

He let go of the shotgun; it clunked against the floor, and he dropped to his hands and knees beside it. Dazedly, he looked toward Cantu, whose shrieking had winded down to silence. At first he assumed the mutant had died from blood loss, but then he saw why he had become subdued. Either accidentally, in falling, or through

Cantu's own actions, the plunger of the syringe in his arm had been depressed and the contents of the barrel flushed into Cantu's vein. He lay on his back staring at the room's fungus-like ceiling, blinking and alive.

"Ohh, dung, what are those?" the mutant slurred. "What the blast are those?"

Malo crawled a little nearer to Zed's feet. There lay the growth he had been about to place into a plastic container. Malo could see its developing limbs waving ever so slightly.

"Thank God," Malo croaked, lying flat on his belly now, reaching out his right hand, pulling the mass toward him. "Thank God you're all right."

He brought the growth close to his face, as if he might kiss its smooth surface to express his gratitude—the way he had gently kissed every inch of Ete-tomi's tattooed, burgundy flesh. And then he bit into it, felt his teeth pop through flesh, felt the tiny limbs bat feebly at his face, felt the gush of fluid jet against the back of his throat.

Still holding the mass to his mouth in both hands, still sucking at its essence, he rolled over onto his back like Cantu, who lay in his spreading pool of blood only a few paces away, the two of them like men on the beds of an opium den.

Flash.

Purple.

Cantu had got there before him, was standing in the same spot where Ete-tomi had stood the last time Malo had come here. The mutant was naked, as was he. In this place, neither of them were marred by their wounds. Cantu stared off toward the horizon . . . awestruck, Malo thought, by the three eggplant-colored moons against the ultraviolet sky, the largest of the trio massive, commanding the heavens. But then Malo realized the man, who he noticed was trembling so hard all over he was positively quaking, was looking up not at the moon but at a creature towering over the two of them. Its legs were so thin, even up close, that Malo hadn't noticed them right away, especially with the dark moons as a background. He did see now, though, the glowing red nodes that marked each joint of those tremendously long, spider-like legs.

Just a few slow-motion strides more, and the thing was right above them. Malo saw two more of them not far behind. Both he and Cantu tilted their heads farther back to gape up at the underside of the creature.

"This isn't real," Cantu chanted, juddering violently but still fixed to the spot where he stood. "This isn't real . . . it isn't real . . . "

"Illusion," Malo told him, "is an illusion."

The creature bent or folded, collapsed or telescoped, one of its limbs in such an unconceivable way that Malo couldn't follow or understand the movement. All he knew was that now, one of those glowing red points on its limbs, resembling a crystal ball filled with blood illuminated from within, was leveled with Cantu's face, only two feet away, as if it were some organ of perception that contemplated him.

"No, no, *no!*" Cantu cried, staring into it, maybe seeing something within the orb that Malo didn't, and then the fleshy nodules atop his head, in their nest of curly black hair, burst all at once. Every one of them, no matter their size. Blood jetted from them in arcs, ran between them in streams down his face and neck. He sank to his knees ... still staring into that red globe ... until he fell forward hard onto his face, which crunched into the soil of the world of the Usumil.

A bluish static flickered into existence, like a phantasmal doppelgänger, superimposed over the dead man.

The limb shifted a little, in that weird way it moved, and Malo felt something like a hot beam of light on his face, though there was no such ray visible ... at least not to his human eyes.

Tears flowed down Malo's face, like the blood that had flowed down Cantu's, but he was smiling when he lifted his arms high to the creature looming far above him.

"I can't go back," he told it. "I'm dead there."

That crystal ball of blood floated nearer to him, and leveled itself with his face.

EMPATHY
Christopher K. Miller

CHRISTOPHER K. MILLER works as a mild-mannered systems programmer through the week but transforms into a super-powered dish washer and egg flipper mornings and weekends for a busy family restaurant. His short fiction includes 7 SFWA sales, mostly to COSMOS, and has appeared in numerous magazines and anthologies, genre and literary, online and in print. His first and only novel, published by a now defunct publisher as an e-book, sold only one copy (to a friend) but was favorably reviewed by both his now deceased parents and ambivalently reviewed by his eldest son. Evidence suggests that Chris is a von Neumann machine.

THEY MET NOT AT ONE OF MEMPHIS'S OVER TWO-THOUSAND

Christian places of worship but at the Cordova Arms-Fair out on Trinity Creek Cove, a few blocks west of the old Walmart supercenter. Sally, who'd driven up from Germantown, was there to return a silencer she'd bought for her T4 Nighthawk. Not defective or anything. Made the 9mm semi-auto's ordinarily sharp report sound to her ears almost exactly like someone coughing spitballs through a fat plastic straw. But it also made poor little Chompy, her Doberman Shepherd cross, yelp and whine, and sometimes even squirt a little, with each wet splut. The sales associate, after explaining the only way Arms-Fair could offer rock-bottom prices on top-of-the-line ordnance was through a strict no-returns policy, admitted someone should've told her that that particular suppressor worked by venting gasses through a kind of ultra-high-frequency whistle. Suggested she try lightening her load, maybe go with the 105-grain Federal Guard Dog round. Safer for shooting home intruders, too. Designed not to punch through walls and such. Even offered to waive commission on a box. But Sally, having already spent over four grand on the premium handgun with optional aluminum frame and padded green carrying case, believed fervently that the store ought to, in her case, make an exception to its strict no-returns policy. Even went so far as to kneel down right there below the week's featured firearm, dubbed Second Amendment, a net-ready, laser-scoped, flash & muzzle-suppressed, self-propelled, .125 cal Barrett/Audi Model 6X6 military-grade sniper rifle with a programmable AI, four integrated 2420p x 1260p 120 fps webcams, a centimeter-level precision Trimble GNSS, and, best of all, remote aim & fire capability. "The drone you own," pitched the display's flawless female voice, engineered to project the same confidence and barely suppressed joy as (but come across a hint less authoritarian than) Walmart's "Please proceed to checkout . . . " lady. Overhead on an airscreen, a 20-point buck nibbled low-hanging acorns in the double crosshairs of a scope whose rangefinder's readout showed 2760' 7.5" through a 2.25 mph east-southeasterly cross-breeze, along with some barometric data. "Hunt anything anywhere from the comfort and safety of your home," prompted the display as Sally closed her eyes, folded her hands, bowed her head and asked Jesus to forgive this salesman his intransigence, show him the error of his ways, and let her at least exchange, if not return, the Osprey.

Jarrod was at an adjacent counter looking to find a choke for the sawed-off Savage-12 he'd just that morning picked up for a song at a lawnsale over in Collierville. Less than a song, even. And for such a beautiful piece: burled black walnut stock with ivory inlay and laser engraving; pristine trigger plate assembly. The seller, some acned kid with a pathological stutter, had been so anxious to part he'd probably have paid to have it taken off his hands. Like an answer to a prayer. Literally. Just not the right answer. Jarrod always prayed before lawnsaling. The counter associate, an older woman with silver hair and a mouthful of gold crowns, agreed it'd be easier and probably cheaper to extend the sawed-off's muzzle with a choke than to try to register it as a short-barrel shotgun. Said she herself had always favored the Cutts compensator. Helluva bang, sure, but no better spread. Too bad they stopped makin em. Smelled of Tennessee corn and sweet pecan bud as she leaned in to whisper he could probably still find used ones on Amazon, though. Otherwise, best go with a Trulock. Lathed solid bar. No welded crap. Jarrod had just fished out his American Express when he saw Sally praying under the soon-to-be-dead buck. Back in a flash, he said, returning the card to its NFC-shielded pouch.

Rang up the devil on his cell, asked how went Emile's first night in the pit. Devil said, Besides someone ate his eyes, seemed to get along.

EMILE, WHO'D BEEN diagnosed with Asperger's syndrome at age five, now, at fifteen, owned more guns than anyone in the store, and maybe the state. He'd memorized all their manuals and could, and regularly did, disassemble, clean, oil and reassemble them in complete darkness. He loved them all. Knew each one's specs—muzzle velocity, recoil energy, target spread and so forth, for every possible load—much the way certain football fans know their favorite teams' passing, rushing, receiving and sack stats, or the way horse racing aficionados tend to know the ponies. In Tennessee, one may not vote or gamble or, in most cases, marry until their late teens, but may, if certified, hunt unsupervised from the age of ten. Emile had received his hunting safety certificate at this tender age and held a valid hunting license ever since. Because he never actually hunted, he needed no special game tags or permits. He was a member of both the Memphis Sport Shooting Association and the Tennessee

Firearms Association, whose magazine, *Sentry*, he always read from cover to cover. Although he did enjoy aiming his firearms via their various aperture, telescopic, holographic and laser sighting mechanisms at shooting complexes' and ranges' NRA-endorsed paper targets and through his bedroom window at unwitting, often moving, targets, and then, when perfectly ready, exhaling a precise and plosive, "bang" or "pow" or, sometimes, "crack" while simulating with his arm and shoulder muscles the weapon's correct recoil, none of his guns had ever actually been fired. His interest in them, though consuming, was purely theoretical in nature.

He had, as per usual, affixed to his person two devices. Beneath baggy fatigues, strapped to his thigh in a custom holster made of old leather belts, was a Glock 18C with a full 33-round magazine and one in the chamber. Though not technically licensed for concealed carry of a machine-pistol, he assumed, given his oft-renewed hunting license, longstanding memberships in the MSSA and TFA, and the numerous caveats in Tennessee's carry laws, that any charges if ever even laid would never stick. Of course he understood himself to be physically and psychologically unprepared to fire it, and really only carried it for the same reason he assumed most civilized nations kept nuclear weapons always at the ready. Strapped to his head was a device resembling a wire-mesh bicycle helmet but that was in fact a low-energy, solid-state maser designed to increase ion-channeling in specific areas of the cerebral cortex, a natural refinement of and extension to the previous century's microwave weaponization and mind-control technologies. It had been prescribed two years ago by a psychiatrist who believed it an efficacious treatment within a narrow spectrum of high-functioning autisms, and always made Emile feel as if he were being watched. There was a panel plate he was not supposed to remove beneath which he'd found a tiny circuit board rife with DIP switches and potentiometers through which he could make adjustments to the unit's demeanor, a demeanor that, for the most part, struck him as benign; interested, but purely as an observer. Although whatever it was stayed always behind him, out of sight, there was a rotary switch that seemed to affect its distance. When screwed full clockwise, it brought the watcher so close as to feel perched on one or the other of his shoulders, evoking images of tiny cartoon devils and angels respectively personifying their characters' ids and super-egos. Counterclockwise seemed to move it back, as much as several yards, and, depending on other settings, could project impetuses ranging from its wishing not to be seen with him to just not being able to keep up. A trio of toggle switches, in one configuration, seemed to augment its default clinical detachment with a sense of bemused curiosity and perplexedness, while, in another, made him feel stalked. Occasionally it would mutter something unintelligible. Asleep, it entered into his dreams but still would not reveal itself, as if even here he could not look upon its face and live. At first it was all very interesting and disconcerting, but over time had become, as long term relationships often do, something he could take for granted and even ignore. But, also as with many long-term relationships regardless of their nurture, he had become addicted to it. Removing the device from his head now made him feel as if, for better or worse, a part of himself were missing, and thereby disenfranchised, unworthy of the universe's attention, so that nowadays, except to make experimental adjustments and, as with the Glock, to bathe or shower, he never took it off.

He'd become something of an Arms-Fair fixture, a valued though standoffish customer who perused the store on a regular twice-daily basis. Naturally he'd discovered a keen interest in the Second Amendment. While drawn, of course, to the rifle's revolutionary specifications and QNX-facilitated integration into the Internet of Things, it was its remote-control enablement that held for him the greatest thrall. Not because it distanced him from the gun but because it distanced him from himself. In effect, let him become the object of his obsession, see the world as if through its eyes instead of his own. Except to blink, breathe and swallow, he'd watched its entire eleven-minute presentation seven times consecutively without employing a single voluntary muscle and could, and did, now mentally recite along word for word with the script's female narrator. When the weapon's high-velocity frangible tungsten-carbide needle struck the 20-point buck just below and behind its right eye, "humanely obliterating its brain," a difficult shot he knew to be discouraged even at much closer ranges, he and his electromagnetic doppelgänger, again, like the buck, though for just that moment, disappeared. This time when he returned, he saw Sally and Jarrod on their knees praying before the sales associate. It was then that the entity strapped to his head demonstrated for the first time a will of its own. In a whisper clear and emphatic, and welcoming of no dissent, it directed that he *join them.*

Told the devil I wouldn't make it, after all. Devil said I shoulda done it when I had the chance.

AT FIRST NEITHER Sally nor Jarrod noticed the young man with the strange crown kneeling behind them. But then both felt something that they would later describe in independent Facebook posts as "an overwhelming sense of forgiveness and reunion."

Sally had always been a Christian and, as such, believed that her belief in Jesus entitled, indeed obligated, her to make requests in his name. It wasn't important to her whether Jesus himself acted directly on her behalf or passed her requests on to God to handle, though her trust in both had been shaken of late.

Jarrod, while more devout, had only been a Christian since college, pursuant to an altar call at a tent revival conducted by a Reverend Roy Jackson, best known for his Southwest radio ministries. It was Jarrod's understanding that invoking Jesus's name authorized him to petition God directly, dropping the son's name serving only as a kind of personal reference or password. His affinity for God had blossomed after losing his own son, Jesse, by neglecting to safety a rifle used to prop a barbed wire fence while out jackrabbit hunting together. He'd bought the gun, a Cricket .22 LR, as a grade 4 graduation present for the boy after seeing it favorably reviewed in a *Field and Stream* article entitled "First Real Rifle" that had rekindled in him some of the excitement of his own first rimfire. In hindsight, he wished he'd taken better note of the reviewer's description of the Cricket's 3-pound trigger pull as "a little light for youngsters." Jesse, who'd not yet taken a certified hunting safety course, had grabbed his new gun by the muzzle after crawling under the wire fence. A sheath of Indiangrass that'd tangled in the trigger guard caused it to discharge.

Not a day, probably not even an hour, had passed since then that Jarrod hadn't played it over in his mind. The pop muffled by Jesse's palm followed by his startled squeak. His own great relief that it was just a small-caliber, copper-jacketed though-and-though, a tiny flesh perforation not much larger than a framing nail would make, and nowhere near any vital organs. Told the kid to wiggle his fingers. No broken bones either. Even made jokes to buck the boy up and staunch his tears while they headed back. Like how many bad guys do you think Roy Rogers shot in the hand? Never aimed to kill, only disarm. Got one almost every episode. Got shot himself in return, too, though. More than a few times. Probably held some sort of record for bullets to the left shoulder. That'd made the kid smile. And didya know him and his wife, Dale Evans, were Christians? Appeared with Billy Graham in crusades all over the country. And didya know it was Mark Twain himself who first called jackrabbits jackrabbits? Before that people called em jack-*ass* rabbits on account of their mule ears. Kid hadn't known any of that. Now Jarrod wished he'd staunched not the boy's tears with jokes and stories but his blood with a tourniquet. Even with the kid wiping it on and sort of hiding it in all that high Indiangrass, like it was an embarrassment, he should've seen, should've taken heed. In hindsight, he always saw clearly: freckles accentuated by the gradual blanching of his son's fair complexion; streaks of crimson in the pale green grass. But not at the time. Not when it mattered, he hadn't. Then, he'd just kept yammering away. Right up until the boy collapsed, and seized. Medical examiner said the bullet had shredded both the superficial and deep palmar arches. A total fluke. Probably couldn't repeat it if you tried a million times. Nonetheless, Jesse, his only son, his best little buddy, had bled out where the wrist's ulnar and radial arteries divide and join in the hand. And no matter how many times and how diligently Jarrod went over it in his mind, revisited and relived the moment and wished and prayed for some other outcome, it always turned out the same. Always the same damn ending.

Sally asked the devil, could she bring a date. Devil said, Sure. Here everybody's welcome.

BACK IN GERMANTOWN, Clarence, Sally's husband of almost thirty years, was dying of pancreatic cancer. He'd refused all treatments save over-the-counter analgesics and prayer, arguing that, given this particular cancer's dire prognosis, he'd probably suffer enough without poisoning, burning and cutting himself all up to boot. Sally'd felt strongly otherwise: that he ought to grab at every available straw, including the Whipple procedure. Of course they'd both asked Jesus for guidance, but apparently gotten different directions. Their insurance provider had raised their deductible even before results from the initial biopsy had come back, so that, had Clarence elected to undergo any of cancer's ghastly and expensive remedies, they would've had to tap out all their credit cards and take out a second mortgage. So, in a way, she'd been relieved by his refusals to submit. Always admired that strong, stubborn streak of his. But now that the cancer had spread to surrounding nerve clusters and the bones of his pelvis and lower back so that he lay in constant and excruciating agony, Sally wondered if Jesus hadn't mistaken her anxieties regarding financial commitments for a want of love and honor, and was punishing her for violating their marriage vows. In any case, it was horrible to behold. Clarence no longer slept as much as just lost consciousness from sheer exhaustion, and even then gnashed his teeth, wept and moaned like the damned. Some people from her church who had their own Facebook group called Prayer Warriors had begun letting her know through daily postings that she and her husband were in their prayers. Sometimes, when Sally was feeling strong and hopeful, she'd ask Jesus for a complete recovery. The rest of the time she just begged for mercy. The Prayer Warriors never said specifically what they were asking for on her and her husband's behalf, and sometimes she wondered if they weren't as ambivalent as she was and if their confusion hadn't caused Clarence to become stuck in the purgatory between life and death, sort of how too many people pushing this way and that on a sofa can get it jammed in a doorway. Or maybe all they asked was God's will be done, which had always struck her as funny in a "goes without saying" kind of way, but now made her angry whenever she stopped to think about it.

Posted on devil's wall, Can we bring the children, too? Devil replied with a like and a smiley: Heavens yes! Wouldn't be the same without em.

EMILE, AFTER TWO years of maser induction therapy, still did not enjoy or encourage the physical proximity of others. His parents, blaming themselves for or just frustrated by his distancing, had compensated by presenting him with a beloved firearm at every gift-giving opportunity, especially Christmas. But now, kneeling behind the pair praying, he experienced an unfamiliar need for closeness. Both disturbing and compelling, it was like the two before him were powerful electromagnets, and he, ferrous metal. As he shuffled forward on his knees into the warmth of their combined auras, the thing that had so long followed behind him now seemed to reach around with appendages that were not so much arms or wings or tentacles but greater extensions of itself, and so more as if to swallow than embrace him. The closer he crawled, the more pronounced this feeling of inclusion became as the more the watcher enfolded itself onto him. When he pulled Sally and Jarrod together and pressed their cheeks to his, the watcher revealed itself in full. And, whereas through the remote-controlled Second Amendment's sensory interfaces he'd become the weapon, here, the weapon became *them*.

Sally and Jarrod's personal space, though diminished, had not been obliterated by their praying together. It was only the spiritual equivalent of sex. So at first it was perturbing to be physically pulled together by this young third party with the strange headgear. But then, whatever it is that distinguishes and separates existence from God and one person from another began to gradually dissolve until they experienced a kind of shared epiphany: that, beyond form's ephemeral distinctions, there is only *one* thing, and that the remote entity, whom they'd been addressing and trying to control through prayer, was in fact themselves.

Jarrod, whose wife had left not long after the death of their son, saw a beloved husband racked by unbearable pain. Remembered a doctor peering up over reading glasses to inform them of his diagnosis: premature menopause. Then, later, a flood of affection at this husband's not caring a whit about any of that. All the more for me, Sweet Pea. Didn't get married to make more people.

And Sally, who'd never had children of her own, saw a beloved son bearing the stigmata. Remembered a Sunday together, after church, plinking at photos of Bin Laden with an air rifle out at the Montgomery County Shooting Complex, and how they'd got into trouble on account of pictures of people weren't allowed as targets there. Almost got the boot. Montgomery's a family-oriented shooting complex with strong Christian values. But then the range supervisor'd laughed and made an exception. Guess if the guy's face is good enough for urinal mats...

And Jarrod realized that the silencer whose return they were praying for wasn't for home intruders at all, but for the beloved husband. That it emended the gun, converted it into a kind of medical device. Just as, Sally now realized, the choke did the sawed-off Savage 12. Together they watched Jesse and Clarence render these purchases immaterial by joining hands across the veil, as they themselves now did around the boy with the funny hat. And Emile, alone at last, reveled in the Second Amendment's looping advertisement's flickering promises, his encroaching sixteenth birthday, and the security of the many straps that now, more than ever, held him together and in place.

Told the devil, Can't stay long. Devil just laughed, handed me a glass and said, Glad you could make it.

THE OBJECT OF YOUR DESIRE COMES CLOSER

Joanna Koch

JOANNA KOCH writes literary horror and surrealist trash. Her short stories have been published in journals such as *Dark Fuse* and *New Millennium Writings*, and in several anthologies including *Doorbells at Dusk*. A Contemplative Psycho-therapy graduate of Naropa University, Joanna lives and works near Detroit. Follow her monstrous musings at horrorsong.blog.

FAY-LIN SWATHED MY BODY WITH BLACK HAIR AND

nervous energy. Barely sated by the last half hour, she spun a thread of hair around her index finger, a spider considering her mate. Happily trapped, sexually inexpert, I waited for the spider to strike. Instead of feeding me poison, she fought to keep me by her side.

I said, "You're the most fearless person I've ever met."

The forerunner of a wrinkle marked her brow. "What you did for us, alone for thirty years, that's true courage, real strength."

I smoothed Fay-Lin's impatient frown with my rough hands, clumsy worship. "Send someone else. You've proved yourself before." Around us, the evidence hummed. Our ill-equipped vessel sailed through the vacuum, eating up space. The unlikely survival of our ship was the last miracle I still believed in: the miracle of Fay-Lin.

"This is different. Damage, some sort of external growth. I don't know what I'm dealing with until I get out on the hull and sample it. Too many unknowns. I need to make decisions in the moment, not manage from a distance."

"Don't go. For me."

Fay-Lin twirled a black lock around her finger. I'd first witnessed this gesture of steeping ire when she was eight. It was our practice as teachers to let the children experience the full consequences of their actions. We stopped short of irreversible damage, but many suffered injuries. They had to learn there were no second chances on an orphaned vessel. At twenty-three, I was an old man to Fay-Lin and a double father figure, both teacher and chaplain. I didn't intervene when her team failed the exercise. She spun a black lock and glared at me as she marched to her simulated death.

My stasis rotation came up soon after. I didn't see Fay-Lin again until we were the same age. I missed watching her grow up. Age twenty-one, ascended to the rank of commander, Fay-Lin woke me to render aid as Minister of the Earth. We were adrift. Food supply ran low. The horror of waking from stasis made me useless to her at first. Some vital part of my soul seemed lost in that long void.

Fay-Lin roused me with her bold touch. How was I to resist? She was my first and only earthly love, though she wasn't born on the earth. Let me say she was my first and only fleshly love.

Our love grew with the crops in the greenhouse. When she revived me, she bade me build a farm from nothing in space. For Fay-Lin, my answer is always yes.

Equal in passion, younger than I am now, I was immune to the mortifications of time. After months of mutual labor and love, I begged her not to send me back to stasis.

"The ship needs me. We can have a life together."

My vows undone, I cared only for Fay-Lin, for the children she might bear me, for her mastery, her courage, for the details of her flesh: the smooth indentation between her breasts that heaved when she was angry or aroused.

"The food supply can sustain itself," she said.

"What about the spiritual needs of the crew. Don't their souls matter to you?"

Fay-Lin caressed me even as she sentenced me to black, undreaming oblivion. "You taught us bodies are compost. Food for the future."

It was true. A large mass of organic material was needed to build the soil for her, to plant. Along with bodily waste and every fleck of carbon and mineral matter at hand, I sought the crew's permission to compost our dead. While I scraped dust and debris from filters, plundered laboratory supplies, and collected personal emissions from all quarters, I rigorously preached the doctrine of ecological fundamentalism.

Sermons subverted the hard fact that someone must dismember our friends, parents, and children. Adding blood, organs and shredded flesh to the bin, monitoring the progress of decay as I aerated, I spared the crew this gruesome task. They saw only the end result: a rich, dark loam.

"Remember," I'd said to Fay-Lin. "The compost runs hot. Bacterial activity accelerates in space. The same might prove true of fungi or some other unknown organism. Who other than me will recognize the signs of imbalance?"

"You have to follow my orders."

"What about you? Don't you need me?"

"That's not the point. If I make one exception, I have to make others."

"I forsook my vows for you."

"You enjoyed every second of it. Report to stasis." She ceased her persuasive caressing. "That's an order."

I'd re-lived our parting endlessly. The pain lingered still as she lay across me now, restless in afterglow, not yet twenty-two. I guess she embraced me to atone, though I was an old man to her again.

While Fay-Lin and the crew had slept in stasis for thirty years, I'd re-established the delicate ecosystem of my misused garden. For Fay-Lin, our fight was months old. For me, it was decades in the past.

I lived and breathed through Fay-Lin. Whether she embraced me out of guilt or nostalgia or obstinance, I cared not. She was mine.

Fay-Lin's cool brow smoothed with certainty. She ceased spinning her black locks and pulled her hair up in a quick knot. She leapt away lightly. I lamented the loss of her weight on my loins.

"Put your vestments on, chaplain," she said, stinging my thigh with a slap. "I need you to pray for me."

FOR MY LOVE, my soul, I sang a Nara period norito. The Shinto gods of ancient Japan were deities of place: mountains, rivers, rocks, and trees. Buddhist statuary technology came later, imposing a human face on the ineffable. As technology proliferated, we put our imprint on the planet, erasing the native face of the land and its many gods. Technology overtook our conscience, and we imprisoned ourselves on this floating world, praying to images both obsolete and out of place.

Did the gods of earth die with our planet? Their voices were silent to me since stasis. I prayed they had preceded us into the void.

Released from the gravity of the ship, Fay-Lin was an acrobat, a spider maneuvering a web of guide lines that might entangle one less deft. She moved like the arborist my parents hired when the trees on earth began dying. I was a child when FEMA declared trees a public safety hazard. Property and persons were at risk from dead, falling limbs. As ecological ministers, my parents refused the municipal utility trucks and hired an older man. He climbed on ropes and worked quietly with a curiously curved, hand-held saw. I followed his ballet in the branches, his intimate dance of canopies and clefts. I spent all day fascinated by the skillful progress of his hopeless task.

Fay-Lin has never seen a tree. She's never lain in the shade and run squealing when a caterpillar dropped on her arm. Or, more like Fay-Lin, she's never climbed too high to negotiate a safe descent, lacked the humility to cry for help, and leapt down to meet her first broken bone. For Fay-Lin, the first of many.

As Fay-Lin examined the hull, the entire waking crew seemed to hold their collective breath. Fay-Lin breathed for all of us in a stream of airy tones over the intercom until disaster ripped the air from our lungs.

The life of the vessel blinked. Orders and expletives flew while back-up power booted with a surge of sound and light. "Hurry, hurry, hurry!" shouted Fay-Lin's second.

"Hold on," she said. "What is this shit?"

"Bring her in," he said. "Now!"

"There's some weird-ass shit all over me, all over the hull—wait—"

"I don't care. Bring her in."

I echoed the second's passion, praying in Greek to disguise my secular intent. Bring her in so she does not sail endlessly into the void. Bring her back, so my soul does not escape. She is my soul, my breath, my life. If this vessel becomes a coffin, let it be a coffin that we share.

The unfamiliar whispers of ancillary power toyed with my ears. I heard an answer in some language older and more arcane than my biblical Greek. The voice was an odd trick of the electronic din. I ceased my prayers and did not hear it again.

"You're under quarantine, commander," said Fay-Lin's second. His name was Salvatore. He was a child of the ship, the same as she.

"Don't be an ass. Open the fucking hatch." Locked in bay twelve, her rig was coated in a sticky phosphorescent material. The substance from the hull had swarmed.

"No can do sweet cheeks."

Fay-Lin punched the door.

Was there more between them than ship's banter? I was an old man from a dead planet. My young shipmates were aliens, creatures reared by space. They didn't care that earth and human history eroded into so much loose debris. They hadn't awoken from their first stasis to a truncated log entry streaming a cataclysm long past.

"We need all non-essential personnel in stasis." Salvatore circled the deck and faced me with his hand upturned like an El Greco masterpiece lost in earth's demise. He had the languid eyes, pale skin and long dark hair of the Spanish renaissance messiah, yet he lacked the experience of seasonal cycles, the basis for understanding the symbolism of resurrection at the heart of all human religions. "Chaplain, please."

"No," Fay-Lin said. "Think about what happened last time he went under. We almost lost our food supply."

Salvatore shot her a cynical look. He sighed. "Chaplain, you understand me, don't you?"

I nodded.

"Permit me to sit with her this one night and offer healing prayers. Tomorrow I'll gladly go. We must conserve resources, after all."

Salvatore squinted in agreement. My relationship with Fay-Lin wasn't a secret.

"Okay. You got one hot priest talking dirty to you all night long, baby. Tomorrow, he's mine."

OVER THIRTY YEARS ago, Fay-Lin sent me away to the horror of dreamless sleep. The garden had flourished. I'd fulfilled her impossible demand. She rewarded me with protocol when I anticipated love. She banished me to that mute hell.

When my stasis was over, I awoke to a crew gone quiet.

The danger of stasis is it deprives the mind of REM sleep. Upon waking, a dreamless brain starts the hard work of hallucination. Dream simulators were in the works when our limited mission ship set out. In dry runs on earth, I suffered minimal detrimental effects. Space changed that. The temporal bound me or betrayed me or—I know not what to say. Some part of my soul went missing in the void.

I awoke to a crew gone quiet and a recorded message from Fay-Lin:

"The crops are failing. We don't know what went wrong. Many starved, stored in cargo three. I don't know if you can use them, if you can do anything. Maybe this is how it ends. Good luck and—" She looked away and then back into the device that imitated my eyes. "You're my only hope. Fay-Lin out."

I played the message again. And again.

Cargo three was like Auschwitz. Heaped bodies, mouths slack, hips splayed by malnourishment. Those I'd birthed, those I'd baptized and counseled; all formless from muscular deterioration, their skin in limpid collapse. Like vampires in a bloodless vacuum, they told the old earth fable of overfeeding and waste. I cried for those I knew, and for the unremembered victims of our planet's history of senseless excess, senseless death.

I toiled in my tainted garden. Some virus or smut had set in. I removed diseased plant material and dumped it through the trash chute. On earth, we burned fields when we needed to purify our land. After burning, the fields were rested. In a canister in space, I could not burn my field. I could only burn time.

Meditation, solitude and fasting were familiar practices to me. Study filled my days. Like slow magic, the soil revived. And shall I confess? The soil recovered more than a decade before I brought the crew back online.

I questioned the morality of aiding a race that destroyed the dwelling place of its gods. I bypassed habitable planets. No spirit dwelled in those places: when I called out to the gods I knew, none answered. I beseeched those unknown, and they denied me discourse. I heightened my study of old languages, seeking the tongue of flame that might ignite a holy fire and force them to speak.

On earth, as a child, the voice of god was always with me. I felt it as presence more than voice, sensation more than words. The voice of god was instinctive and intimate, a part of my body. When it grew small, I journeyed into field or forest until it spoke and held me close again.

Earth's varied lands had different deities, different dialects, yet the unity and wholeness of nature aligned with one voice. Abandoned in space, I longed for that oneness.

A rustling like the softest breeze shimmering in many leaves lingered beneath the engine's hum. Like the sacred singing of trees, like canopies animated by wind, a subtle chorus hinted joy. I prayed in darkness to increase my aural sensitivity. I doubled the length of my fasts and gave up all bodily comfort. I stopped praying after some time and only listened, my eyes hooded, my knees cramped. The suggestion of a voice slid across the edge of my perception like the sound of a shadow. Excited, I resolved to remain cloistered until the voice of god revealed itself.

When it—they—spoke to me, I snatched off my hood. I dared not listen in the dark. They were not one, but many.

The voices of the new gods whispered of unseen things embedded in the air, of worlds folding like diseased proteins, of minds and wills without place seeding themselves in human tissue like maggots born in meat. They lacked the presence of my earth gods and exuded a palpable absence. They took my memories away and gave them back changed. Sunlight was not the life-giving glow that filtered into the earth's atmosphere and nourished her lush growth; sunlight was a fire, a nova, a radioactive chain of gaseous explosions. From the perspective of space, my concept of sunlight was romance, my feelings delusions.

The new gods whispered to me. They lured me with their languages. Seduced by their tutelage, I soon whispered back.

The languages felt slippery, like oysters on my tongue. I understood few words, and grasped their impact by transcribing syllables into the perverse hieroglyphs demanded by such suggestive tones. Sickened and aroused by images of sexual carnage and hypocritical sadism, I hardly believed I'd composed them. The contortions of the written symbols disturbed me more than their alien sounds. I argued with the darkness that seeped from every crevice of the ship. I rubbed my flesh raw with incessant desire as the voices crept inside me from the void. Their bubbling and clicking wormed its way into my memories and dreams. I found no refuge in replaying the message from Fay-Lin. They fondled me in my nightmares, filling me with hot pleasure and burning disgust.

Born a Minister of the Earth, I refused to die a scribe to the gods of no-place. I brought the crew online.

Three decades had passed. My clothes were rags. Unshorn hair clumped in knots. My forehead was striped by scars—had I clawed at my eyes against the atrocities I transcribed? The blood caked beneath my nails proved it true. I looked in the mirror, and a demon ogled back. Burst blood vessels branched towards black, dilated discs. Dead suns set in the center of my eyes. These twin witnesses shed no human light. They sucked at my sanity with confusion and cruelty. A feral language had fed upon my soul.

The miracle of Fay-Lin saved me from the mad black hole

imploding my pupils. She silenced the uncouth ramblings of the new, revolting gods. She cleansed and cared for me, and filled me with sunlight. How fitting that now Fay-Lin emitted her own ephemeral light, quarantined by the slimy bioluminescence adhering to her skin. I sat with her, gazing through the window of the medical bay where she'd been transferred. Tests were inconclusive. Her body glowed like a creature from the sea.

I had no intention of being banished into undreaming silence, or worse, locked away with the voices of wrong, alien gods in perverted darkness. My salvation tied me to Fay-Lin. Thus, at the first opportunity, I broke quarantine and entered the medical bay where she was confined.

WHAT IS THE form in a soul that seeks to be formless? What is the voice that speaks in languages we do not know? Whence comes the knowledge that deciphers the unknown tongue and tastes its thoughts? Whose are the teeth that bite off the tongue and swallow it like a wormy delicacy, an infernal morsel? Mine. Always mine, for I do all that the goddess requires of me, no matter the cost.

Fay-Lin grew buds. Long, stringy nodules propagated from her extremities. Physicians' orders said to cut them off. To me, the fibrous, searching nature of the nodules suggested intelligent tropism rather than disease. I allowed one foot to grow and kept it hidden from the medical staff.

"Thirsty," Fay-Lin said. Her flesh pulsed with indescribable colors. Her movements grew imperceptibly slow. Her body seemed stiff, but I observed she remained pliant to the touch. Her position hardly changed from hour to hour, and the sluggishness of her jaw allowed only a liquid diet. Her thirst was unquenchable.

I remained immune. Outside the medical bay, many suffered contamination. Conditions were far from ideal for controlling infection, and medical care spread thin. Allowed enough neglect for an experiment, I served Fay-Lin her next liquid meal by immersing her tendril-covered foot in the drink.

She hummed with relief.

Patients dehydrated. Infection spread. An attempt to share my discovery was rewarded by expulsion from Fay-Lin's cell. I was escorted forcefully to stasis. With every step further from Fay-Lin, the infernal voices spread.

I could not bear the slimy, awful pressure of their sinister whispers. I was a peaceful man. The familiar suggestiveness of their unknowable words prodded at my sanity. I commanded them to stop. I screamed. I tore at them, fought and ripped and railed against them with tooth, nail, and fist. They ceased, I gave thanks, and my escort lay beneath me, mangled about the face and neck, gurgling as he tried to call out an alarm. I broke his arm, I think, with my boot. When I left him he was quite still.

I rescued Fay-Lin from starvation. The physician was an obstacle easily overcome. Love moved me with the strength of worship. I lifted Fay-Lin with little effort despite my lack of training and my age. Her eyes were wide upon me as I carried her away.

On earth, in spring and summer, one might lie beneath a tree captured by the glory of the light streaming through lofty branches. In fall, leaves turned gold. Sacred decay of the sinking sun gilded each dead leaf like a pharaoh's sarcophagus shimmering in the water as it drifted down the Nile. Perhaps I missed the wind more than any other element on earth. Fay-Lin was stiff yet supple, and I wished for the elements to move her, touch her, and pleasure her. My clumsy flesh lacked the sensitivity of the breeze that once brushed the high trees with erotic abandon.

In her altered state, I could not touch Fay-Lin in the correct way. But I could plant her.

ONCE, WHILE HIKING with my parents, fall had come too soon. Adults said the untimely seed heads and brittle grasses were proof of climate change. I lagged, a dreamy boy enamored by some bramble or pod. Their voices vanished on the breeze, and a strong gust grabbed the landscape and shook all the scrub around me. Dead and dying flowers rattled and shuddered with delight. They raised a mighty choir in the wind: *We are going to seeeed!*

I rushed to tell my parents the good news: earth was happy for her death, ready to complete her cycle and go to seed. I'd forgotten this early memory until today, when I saw the new life taking root around me. We've been foolish to try to impose our human face on another world, vain to view our drifting selves as anything other than seeds.

The ship glows and pulses as components assimilate with bioluminescent life. It is an organism, a floating temple to the goddess

Fay-Lin. Her wild eyes watch as I harvest unbelievers and add them to the soil. Her eyes grow wet as she witnesses the miracle of her own rebirth. I prune her limbs and root them in the loam. One becomes many. Fay-Lin is a grove of infinite goddesses. Her cuttings take on strange and wondrous forms. Each is a unique, unpredictable body of flesh, tooth and thorn. Some lack symmetry or turn inside out as they flower. Most produce fruit, though it is hard to pluck. She guards the harvest with stinging tendrils and snapping mouths.

The hair of Fay-Lin trails high into the alcove above the greenhouse. Black locks twist with autonomous intelligence. I often wake cradled in their silk. It is soothing to be lifted, rocked and spun, but I must forego such indulgence. I'm tasked to replenish the soil. I pray the organic matter on hand will create the self-sustaining rhythm of a forest. I peel away her sticky threads and climb down from her black, creeping filaments. Where she has swathed my skin, it tingles.

Fay-Lin's strong trunk sprouts new growth from old wounds. The mystery of her flesh blooms in a kaleidoscope of impossible colors. Where I prune one limb she grows many. Where I cut again, she leafs out in a flush of gelatinous light. She watches me lovingly with the weak relics of her human eyes. When I rest the head of Salvatore in her roots, she seems intent to speak.

The many voices of Fay-Lin, like the many eyes glowing from her forehead, thrill my soul like no deity bound by place. New rows of eyes increase in a luminous spectrum of black, their colors swirling like oil. Spider mother, tree mother, goddess of the floating garden between worlds, Fay-Lin reveals herself as the oldest deity of earth.

She left before written history, before language. How long has she waited for us to follow her into the void? She is the goddess of the hunt who takes her chosen son as consort and priest.

Her voice is inside me, like the sap in a sapling. I minister to her large, hungry limbs, strange organs that terminate in a radius of starry tentacles. Small suction cups on their undersides pull me in where she hides a hot liquid that bathes me in unbearable pleasure. Her branches curl around my thrusting body, changing shape as they fit my form. I shudder and scream the obscene words of her hieroglyphs. Black sap pumps out of me with holy fury.

Our offspring shiver with shared delight. They rattle, though there is no breeze. They sprout fast, feast on rich soil, and grab the raw meat from the compost with impatient vines. I tend this bloody temple, this vessel like a womb that birthed my soul when I thought she was forever lost. Here, I commit my aging body to the soil. The day comes closer when I feed the sacrament of my death to the void for all eternity.

THE SECOND ISSUE OF

SYNTH

WILL BE PUBLISHED

JUNE 15, 2019

With new stories by

Tim Major
Casilda Ferrante
Dan Stintzi
Stephen Oram
Selene dePackh
J.T. Glover
Tim Jeffreys
Zandra Renwick

www.synthanthology.wordpress.com

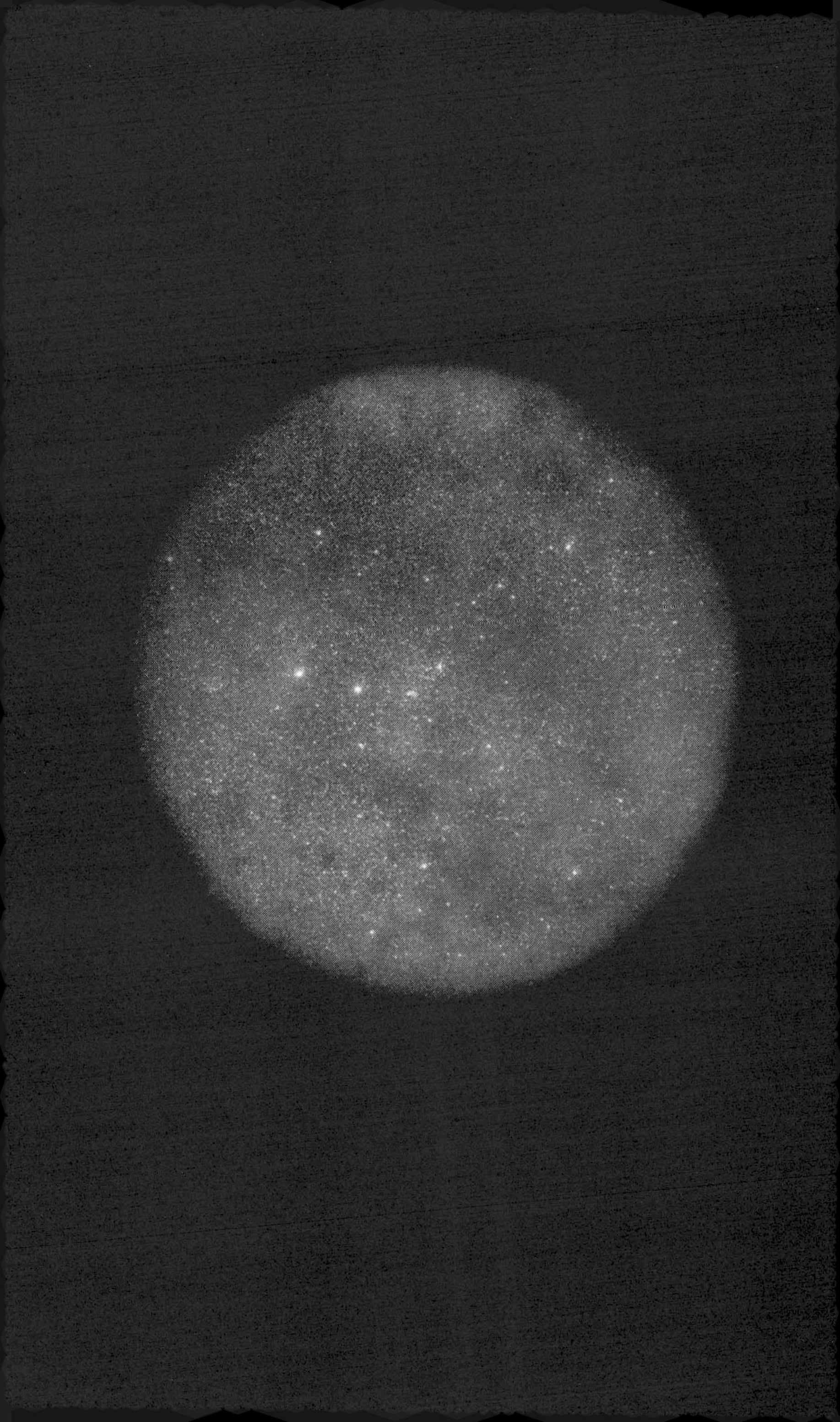

Made in the USA
Middletown, DE
26 March 2019